am

FATAL
IMPRESSIONS
□□□□□□□□□□□□□□□■

Also by Wayne Warga
HARDCOVER

FATAL IMPRESSIONS

□□□□□□□□□□□□□□■

Wayne Warga

Arbor House | William Morrow
New York

Library of Congress Cataloging-in-Publication Data

Warga, Wayne.
        Fatal impressions / Wayne Warga.
                p.   cm.
        I. Title.
        PS3573.A755F3 1989   88-29061
        813'.54—dc 19   CIP
        ISBN 0-87795-990-0

Printed in the United States of America

First Edition

1 2 3 4 5 6 7 8 9 10

BOOK DESIGN BY MINA GREENSTEIN

This book is for
Mike Franzblau, Joe Jares,
and David Lewis—friends indeed

FATAL
IMPRESSIONS
□□□□□□□□□□□□□□■

□□□ 1 ∎

IT NEVER got easier. The flat cardboard storage folder, as usual, measured five feet by five. This was his fifth. And with all of them he'd set out fortified by several martinis and a fistful of red downers. To judge from his record, he should have been more calm. Six arrests and one conviction for breaking and entering, five more arrests but no convictions for drug dealing. This was by far the oddest encounter of his career. So damned conspicuous, yet so easy. As instructed, he wore a suit, and as he trudged down Fifty-seventh Street bearing his unwieldy package, he pretended to be casually inspecting the art-gallery windows. He looked as though he were wandering. What he really was doing was wondering what such a job would be worth the next time. He intended to raise the price. A brisk blast of New York winter wind blew through his topcoat. He shuddered and buttoned it, never for a second relaxing his grip on the big folder. It was cold, but he could feel himself sweating.

He came to the address he had memorized, stepped

out of the street traffic, hitched the folder up under his arm. He passed easily through the door and signed in with the inattentive guard, just as he had been told to do. The guard made note of his big folder, but little else. A man with such a folder was commonplace in a place like this. He joined the stream of people on their way to an opening, which was on the third floor. He pretended he could not fit into the small elevator with them, shrugged genially, and started up the stairs. He climbed all the way to the seventh floor. He had already been told there would be no alarm system. It took him less than two minutes to pick the locks on the side door leading into the gallery. Once inside he saw a light had been left on. He wouldn't need the high-beam pencil light in his pocket.

He found what he was looking for in the top row of storage bins near the gallery owner's office. There were twelve folders in all, so he counted to seven and pulled one out. The label on it said THEN CAME AN OX AND DRANK THE WATER. He opened it, then untied the strings on his folder and opened it as well.

He stood before a riot of color, form, and design. He bent down and compared the signatures and numbers on both. Each bore the same inscription: 21/60 F. STELLA '84. He now knew what that meant: number twenty-one out of an edition of sixty prints, signed and dated by Frank Stella. Before him was an original and a forgery from Stella's illustrations after El Lissitzky's *Had Gadya*. He hadn't any idea who El Lissitzky was, what the *Had Gadya* was, but he did know who Frank Stella was: Frank Stella was money. He had made sure of that just after he did the first job. He had gone down to SoHo to the Castelli gallery and inquired about the works of Frank Stella, in particular about the artist's newest prints from the *Had Gadya*. He was not all that surprised to learn each print in the series of twelve was selling for $25,000. Selling, that is, when one could be located. Demand had immediately outstripped the supply.

With great care he removed the light tape holding the forgery in its case, laid it on the adjoining tabletop, and even more carefully—no tear in the tape could show—extracted the original from its taped mooring. It was less than ten minutes from the time he entered the gallery to the time he left.

The rendezvous was set for an hour later along the old shipping docks on the West Side. He had time for a few drinks, so he set out for a bar close by where he was to meet the well-dressed man with the slight accent who had promised him $5,000 for exchanging the series of prints in three different Manhattan galleries. He didn't know the man's name—certain information wasn't exchanged in bargains like this—but he already had half the money and had been told he would have the rest tonight. The bar was a hangout for derelicts, so he found an empty booth, placed the folder opposite him, and ordered the first of four double shots of bourbon and water. Then he left.

"Get in."

"What?" The booze and pills were taking their toll, and he wanted his money quickly so he could buy a few lines of cocaine before he called it a night.

"I said get in." There was only a slight hint of impatience.

He heard the door locks on the Mercedes sedan snap open, so he opened the rear door and started to place the original print on the backseat. His patron got out to help him slide the big folder in. He started to open the front passenger's door, but he never made it.

The soft pop of the silencer was drowned by the rush of traffic on the West Side Highway above. The man was an expert shot: The bullet entered the thief's brain through the back of his skull and killed him instantly. The driver quickly stooped down and patted the man's body for identification. As he suspected, there was none. He pulled the body into the entrance of an alley, then drove off.

Finding a body in an alleyway of one of New York's seamiest neighborhoods was a usual occurrence. Finding the body of a man with a record of arrests for drug dealing was even more routine. The police may have wondered why he was wearing a suit and a tie, but it was a minor speculation. When routine inquiries produced nothing by way of new information, the murder was written off as just another bloody incident on the long, long list of drug-related deaths.

2 ∎

"NO, NO. A little bit more to the right." Her long index finger was poised thoughtfully on her lips, a sure sign of deep concentration. She was going to get it right, or else.

"Now?" Jeffrey's arms were aching. The print and its heavy frame measured four by four and it was even heavier than it looked. Holding it up for more than a few moments was nearly impossible. "Quick, make your marks or I'll drop it."

She took the broken pencil stub and reached in behind the print, using the two circular hook anchors as her guide. She put a small mark on the wall where they would match into the hooks. "There!" She helped him rest the print on the floor.

"Shall I?" He was smiling, two nails sticking out of his mouth, a hammer in his hand.

"Why don't I?" she responded diplomatically. He handed her the hammer but refused to release the nails until she had patted him softly on the lips. She expertly hammered the nails into the wall, exactly on the pencil marks.

Rachel did things exactly. Jeffrey was less exact, and considerably less patient. Putting up the track lighting in the living room had caused him fits of anger frequently during the afternoon and she was determined to head off any more explosions. They had worked hard all day, happily indoors out of the rain, which was pouring steadily over all of Los Angeles. It was, after all, their home and their living room, and they were making it exactly as they wanted it. Rachel more exactly than Jeffrey.

She was on the ladder, balancing a level between the two hooks, leaning over to make sure the little bubble was in the middle. She was wearing paint-smeared jeans and one of Jeffrey's old button-down shirts, which also bore considerable evidence of her industriousness with a paintbrush. He was similarly dressed and stained, though a good bit messier. He watched her and smiled, then reached up slightly to slide his hand up inside her shirt, gently stroking her breasts. She smiled down at him, then pushed his hand away.

He had never been so happy. So much had changed these last few years since they had met. Jeffrey Dean Rare Books had become such a successful business that he had dutifully incorporated under the laws of California, the better to shelter his income. She, meanwhile, had abandoned her job as a teacher of freshman English, gone back to school and finished her master's degree in fine arts, and was just a dissertation short of her doctorate. All that and she had worked part time in a gallery and had then, just a year ago, opened her own art gallery in the empty store beneath Jeffrey's office.

They had bought the house seven months ago, and energetically plunged into the trap set by the real estate agent, who had described the house as "an easy fixer-upper." It hadn't been easy, but it was turning out to be

worth both the work and the expense. The old run-down
Spanish-style house in the Sherman Oaks hills had under-
gone a methodical metamorphosis. First the kitchen had
been rebuilt, then the hardwood floors refinished. Doors
had been replaced, windows repaired, the Spanish tile
roof made leakproof, and the house itself painted. Finally,
it was time to paint the inside. This they decided to do
themselves, mostly to save money.

"Ready," she said. It wasn't a question. Together they
lifted their prize and hung it on the wall. They stood back
and gazed, their arms around each other, her head resting
lightly on his shoulder. She had literally stayed awake
nights debating whether or not to buy it. He had slept
soundly, his decision made. It was Frank Stella's newest
lithograph, one from his *Had Gadya* series. They had
chosen the eighth print in the series, *The Butcher Came
and Slew the Ox*. Although it was a print it nevertheless
seemed to possess a third dimension. It defied con-
ventional shape, literally jumping out of the confines of
its borders, themselves defying containment. Its colors
were varied and rich, its details precise. It was, she was
certain, the best print of the whole series. Stella's work
seemed to soar, and it was as though they had bought the
brightest, most joyously uninhibited print of them all.
Her certainty was informed and educated. His was vis-
ceral. Once the decision was made there was only one
barrier to hurdle. The cost. They had intended to wait at
least a year before buying art, but it just hadn't worked
out that way.

Jeffrey began gathering up the drop cloths and empty
paint buckets. She used a clean towel to remove their fingerprints from the glass over the print, then began putting the furniture back in place. There wasn't much, and
it didn't take long. She was adjusting the Oriental carpet
in front of the fireplace, struggling to line it up exactly on

the padded liner beneath it, when Jeffrey reappeared with a bottle of wine and two chilled glasses.

"I think I'm in love," Jeffrey said, opening the wine.

"You'd better be." She smiled at him. "You can't afford anything else, and neither can I. We're going to have to live on love now."

"Somehow," he said, looking around the room at their sparse collection of furniture, "I don't feel like I'm broke." There wasn't much, but it was all good, all carefully chosen. None of it had been cheap.

Rachel had adroitly mixed contemporary furniture with the old-style architecture and the result was both warm and luxurious. She stretched, sat down on the sofa, and carefully pulled two books from beneath the cushion beside her. They had put them there while they painted. Both were first-edition Charles Dickens and very rare. One was a copy of *The Personal History of David Copperfield*, and the other was *The Life and Adventures of Nicholas Nickleby*, inscribed to a friend by Dickens himself. They were treasures in the eyes of any bibliophile, and normally Jeffrey believed in selling his treasures. It was, after all, his business. But not these two books. They were personal treasures as well, brought back from London in their hand luggage, smuggled past an unsuspecting customs inspector. They were from another time and another place, and for Jeffrey and Rachel they were also mementos of their own private beginning.

Jeffrey took the books from her and placed them between two antique marble bookends that sat on the reading table beside his favorite chair. Then he put a match to the gas jet in the fireplace and started the fire.

They sat on the sofa, sipping their wine and admiring their Stella, blissfully unaware that they looked like two splattered house painters sitting in their employer's living room admiring their handiwork. The fire popped, and the rain splattered the big living-room window. Sounds that soothed.

"You want some dinner?" she asked.

"Maybe some soup later."

"Some hot tea?"

Jeffrey shrugged, undecided.

"Me?"

"Tea or you? That's an interesting choice."

She smiled.

"Well, whichever is easier to make."

She feigned disapproval, sat for a second, then stood and took a pillow from the sofa and put it on the rug before the fire. She unbuttoned her shirt and took it off, tossing it into a corner of the room. Her jeans and underpants followed.

"Thanks, but I think I'll just watch," Jeffrey said, sipping his wine.

She stretched and waited, all the time watching him, almost daring him. Jeffrey stood, undressed, and knelt beside her. With his left hand he caressed her cheek, with his right he gently pulled her knees apart and began by kissing the inside of her thighs.

□□□ **3** ■

THE GALLERY was located on Michigan Avenue north of the Chicago River in the stratospheric rent district. Everything, he had been told, was arranged. It had worked twice before, so why not this time?

Workmen had begun unstringing the white Italian lights that decorate Michigan Avenue during the holidays, leaving half of the bare trees unlit, the rest sparkling brightly. Pedestrian traffic was sparse, and no wonder. An icy, piercing Chicago wind was blowing full force off of Lake Michigan. Holding on to the large folder was a challenge, and he succeeded only by walking into the wind and letting the package bend slightly against him. He knew if he held it wrong it would become like a sail, and he would be racing along the icy sidewalk until he fell and ruined everything.

The building contained an auditorium, and inside the lobby people were waiting for a chamber-music concert to begin. He walked in, stepped into the elevator, and when he saw he was alone, decided to ride it to the floor

MADISON COUNTY
LIBRARY
S · Y · S · T · E · M

This receipt is your official notice of
the due dates of the items you have
checked out. Any email or phone
reminders are for convenience only.
All items not returned or renewed
by the specified dates will be
subject to fines.

DATE DUE RECEIPT

User name: GILL, RODRIQUEZ

Title: Fatal impressions
Author: Warga, Wayne.
Item ID: 31776000242618
Date due: 11/26/2011,23:59

mángo.
languages

Try Mango, our free online language learning
resource. Learn Spanish, French, Italian,
German, Japanese, and English!

he wanted. What the hell. He had been instructed to get off two floors above his destination, but who would know? He was cold and his fingers, which were crucial to his work, were frozen stiff inside his gloves.

He found the gallery door, then set to work with his pick, working it into the lock to accomplish what the serrations and warding of a real key would do. The first lock gave way easily, the second resisted, then tumbled on the third try.

The alarm system was unsophisticated and easily jammed. He had been told to expect it and also exactly what to do. It had a thirty-second delay before going off, so that the owner could get inside and shut it down. The art storage bins were to the right, off the small lobby. He stepped inside, closed the door, and switched on the light.

The exchange was simple. The original was loose in its large folder, so he pulled it out and looked at it quickly, comparing it to the forgery. He couldn't tell them apart. He read the signatures on both. The original was print number fourteen of sixty. His contact had made a mistake. The forgery was number thirty-four of sixty. A quick search of the storage bin proved it wasn't in this gallery. Imagine, sixty of them—all candidates for a switch with a forgery. He tried to compute a price for the total, and quickly gave up. A lot, he was certain of that. He grabbed the thin catalog sitting on the shelf by the stored prints and looked up the print by matching the colors. It was *Then Came Death and Took the Butcher*.

He thought for a moment, decided the gallery owner would probably consider the new number a mistake he had made in his filing system when the print arrived. That is, if he noticed the error at all. He made the switch, carefully tied the original into his folder, and left.

It was even colder back on Michigan Avenue. He considered taking a cab to the meeting place, but decided it was too risky. A man with a large folder picked up on Michigan Avenue when there were no other people about would be remembered. The scar on his chin—from a prison fight—was easily identifiable. He pulled up the collar of his coat and began the walk to North Clark Street.

It was on the edge of skid row, a street of bars and drinkers by day and littered with drunks by night. He bent into the wind and waited in the doorway of a Japanese hardware store, where it was nearly impossible to see him from the street. The folder was behind him, pressed against the wall.

He glanced up and down the street, suppressing his anxiety. Tonight was his last delivery, and tonight the payoff was due. Ten minutes later the Mercedes with the New York license plates passed once, slowed, then came around the block again. He stepped to the curb. The car stopped and the driver, a well-dressed blond man who spoke with a slight accent, stepped out, pulling on his gloves.

"Did it go well?"

"Yeah. Except somebody fucked up."

The man stiffened, and the thief could see his blue eyes glitter in the cold. "What are you saying?"

"The print in the gallery was number fourteen of sixty. The fake was number thirty-four."

"I see. But you made the exchange anyway?"

"Yeah. I figured the gallery people would think they had written the wrong number on their inventory."

"Good. Here, let me help you."

He opened the rear door, then stood aside so that the thief, who was now shivering from the cold, could slide the folder into the car. As he bent over to give it a final push, he felt the cold grip of strong hands on his neck and a knee in the small of the back. Before he could protest, death came and took the thief. There was a muffled crack as his spine snapped from the pressure and a small gasp as his last breath strangled into his throat and formed a small cloud of mist in the freezing air. The driver shoved his body into the backseat and quickly drove off.

The next morning a frozen nude body was found just a few blocks away floating in the Chicago River. It was eventually identified as a thirty-four-year-old Vietnam veteran with a record for armed robbery. The police were accustomed to finding corpses in the river, and since it was a man with an arrest record and one prison sentence, they made relatively little note of it. The incident was entered into their computer, remained active for a short time, and was then filed into storage with hundreds of others.

□□□4∎

IT WAS catalog time, which meant Jeffrey's usual calm demeanor was subject to brief eruptions. He compiled his lists at least four times a year, mailed them out to his customers and prospective customers, then sat back and waited for the telephone to start ringing. It always did, setting off a flurry of packing and mailing. It seemed to him to become more tedious each time he did it, but he knew too that—like almost all rare-book dealers—he would be out of business if he didn't do it. The bulk of his income came from the meticulously written descriptions of books.

His word processor was humming and he was on item seventy-five, an inscribed copy of E. M. Forster's *A Room with a View*. Forster inscriptions to his readers were rare, inscribed copies of this particular novel even rarer. So rare Jeffrey couldn't even find the book on his shelves when he went to match the description with the book itself. Somehow, he thought, it had been misfiled, and he wasn't certain of the publication date.

He searched for several frustrating minutes, cursed, then stepped into the small kitchen of what had once been his apartment and was now part of the newly expanded office of Jeffrey Dean Rare Books. What had originally been his bedroom and living room—back in what he thought of as the pre-Rachel years—were now also lined with shelves. He glared at the rows of books, then turned on the tea kettle. He entertained comforting thoughts of finding an eager library-sciences student at UCLA and hiring him to prepare his catalogs.

With growth—and it had been just short of phenomenal—had come change. And with change in an otherwise orderly life, had come the inevitable confusion. Sipping his tea, he surveyed the shelves once again.

"You son of a bitch, there you are." He found it exactly where it belonged, alphabetically filed with a dozen or so other books that needed double-checking before they could be entered into the catalog. He checked the date—1908—and the price—$750—smiled, and walked back into the kitchen.

When he heard the slap of the mail in his downstairs mailbox, he jumped from his word processor and started down the stairs. Halfway down he remembered it was Monday: Rachel's gallery was closed, so he needed to collect her mail as well. He turned back to get her keys out of his desk.

Customers were lining up for lunch at the chic bistro across the old brick walk outside his door. No doubt about it, the San Fernando Valley—at least this little corner of it—was becoming extremely fashionable. The increase in rents proved it. So did the increase in crowds. He had a long-term lease at a reasonable rent. Rachel, coming along several years later, had fared less well with their landlord. Still, she was making it—just.

He looked into the window of the gallery. Four paintings hung on the white walls, all by young, relatively unknown Los Angeles artists. He knew they were installed only temporarily, but nevertheless they looked very good. The big show, the one they both fervently hoped would be Rachel's first major impact on the rapidly expanding art community of Los Angeles, was still five days away. Both of them were anxious about the show, eager to get it hung. Soon. Rachel, who would normally appear after lunch on Monday to work on her account books, was at the printer, riding herd on the color plates being extracted from her catalog to be given clients as business cards.

Neither Jeffrey nor Rachel spent much time reflecting on the many changes in their lives—in part because change has its own momentum and also because, as basically thoughtful people, they had become caught up in it. Now their lives were about to change again, and once again for the better. It had begun more than a year before with a telephone call from Rachel, who was in New York.

Lena Sabin, the five-foot-one towering legend of the rare-book world had, at age eighty-six, died. Died, Jeffrey had remarked at the time, in a way that suited her perfectly. She had been in London, wheeling and dealing, and was on her way to still another in her endless list of meetings, when she made the typically American error of looking the wrong way before crossing a street. A truck had struck her and she died instantly. Lena had introduced Jeffrey to Rachel, who was her niece, and once Jeffrey and Rachel's worlds had merged she had loved them both equally and generously. And why not? The crafty old woman could see that her business expanded considerably with Rachel and Jeffrey on the West Coast and her in New York. Not so much holding forth as reigning, she carried on the business she and her late husband had begun when they were penniless refugees from Hitler's Germany. Lena was childless, and Rachel was her sole heir. When she died, Jeffrey and Rachel knew they would inherit her big book collection, and she had been very specific about what to do with it. Sell it, she said, to the highest bidder. Some might have wanted such a collection to go to a library, with suitable immortalization and a fancy plaque implied. Not Lena. Her sense of immortality was rooted firmly in commerce. Rachel's call from New York, and her astounding news, was something neither had anticipated, Lena having—as usual—kept her secret to herself.

Lena and Ben—who had died twenty years before—had not emigrated penniless after all. They had been part of Berlin's society of artists and writers, and had joined the exodus when the Nazis rose to power. Among their friends—and fellow émigrés—had been George Grosz, the artist whose satiric drawings had impaled the National Socialists with a sharp and telling wit. Grosz was already famous when he left Germany, and his fame increased when he began painting in America. With this came a marked increase in value, and Lena had fourteen of his works tucked away in storage: three paintings of luscious Grosz women, and eleven drawings, ranging from Berlin men with their women to the political satire that had brought Grosz his initial fame—and notoriety—in Germany.

"I always told you she was a great gossip, but also a great keeper of secrets," Jeffrey had told Rachel when she telephoned.

"Now I believe you. This is incredible," Rachel said, her voice catching. She was caught in the dilemma of sincere grief mixed with great surprise.

"You always wondered why she approved of your

going back to school to study art history instead of staying in the book business or teaching. Now you know."

"And I know why she always took me to the Museum of Modern Art when I was little, and why she always stopped for the longest time in front of the Grosz works. Especially after Uncle Ben died. They were her touchstones. That, and her books."

Lena Sabin's books—some five hundred of them—and her Grosz art were now all in Los Angeles. Jeffrey had agreed to sell the books, but insisted on handing over all profits to Rachel's gallery. It was an offer Rachel had refused flat out, and for two reasons. She wanted to respect Lena's wishes, and she wanted Jeffrey to share in her own good fortune. It had taken a good bit of convincing, but Jeffrey had finally agreed.

The books were in cartons at their house. The works by George Grosz were in Hollywood at an expert framer. One of the paintings—a pink-cheeked, plump prostitute sitting before her mirror applying her makeup, and naked except for black stockings—would eventually be hung in their home. So would one of the most pointed of the satirical drawings. The rest, as Lena specified in her will, were to be sold. Jeffrey and Rachel planned to hang them in Rachel's gallery that next day. The show was to open Friday night.

It was Jeffrey, with his knowledge of journalism and the implicit rules of publicity, who had come up with the master stroke:

"Give one of the best drawings to the County Museum as a gift in Lena's name. You'll create goodwill, you'll have access to expert advice, you'll get loads of publicity. And you'll be in business for good."

Rachel had readily agreed.

□□□ **5** ∎

THE NIGHT air along the beach was almost tangible, a dense fog that enveloped the few people walking along the boardwalk. He had planned it this way: approach the gallery from exactly the opposite direction of all the others, who were held up in heavy traffic as the city's boulevards and freeways compacted onto the narrow beach roads.

He was dressed to mix in unobtrusively with the crowd. His blazer, open-necked shirt, and casual demeanor rendered him effectively indistinguishable from the others circulating around the inside of the gallery and spilling out on the sidewalk in front of it, plastic wineglasses in their hands and a look of nervous anticipation on their faces. Like most of their kind, they were looking to find others they already knew. It was an insular and incestuous crowd, one given to ignoring strangers.

His large folder containing the three Stella forgeries was sitting in a janitor's closet at the opposite end of the gallery. He had put it there during the last-minute flurry

of work before the show started, entering through the
rear door while the caterers were setting up. It had been
easy.

The first two switches had been easy also, both inside
closed galleries in the middle of the night. This was beginning well too, but it needed the sort of daring that
invariably made him nervous. He preferred to work
alone and away from a crowd. He considered this grand-
standing, but since the pay was $5,000 for the three jobs,
he'd damn well do it nude if that's what the German
wanted.

He thought the German was weird because he was
involved with art and art galleries. He had read from time
to time of the large amounts of money involved in art
dealing, but reading it did little to curb his skepticism.
Still. He put his wine down on the bar untasted, and
moved toward the back of the big exhibit room. He pretended to be looking at a painting—he thought it was
terrible, even though the eccentrically dressed fat woman
standing near him was making clucking noises of approval. What the hell. He had observed the parade of
Mercedeses, BMWs, and Jaguars pulling up to the valet
parking. These people had the money to buy this stuff.
As for him, he was a cat burglar, and right now he was
prowling in public. He didn't like that at all. Better to get
it done and get the hell out of this place.

When he felt no one would notice, he stepped around
the bar and walked down the short hallway. If he was
stopped he would say he was looking for the bathroom.
The large storage room was open, its floor littered with
open cartons of wine bottles and empty hors d'oeuvre
platters. He slid the flat folder out of the janitor's closet,
knocking over a mop in the process. He stepped across
the hall to the storage room and quickly set about making
the switch. All three prints he carried were the same. All

by Frank Stella: *Then Came a Dog and Bit the Cat*. He closed the door, looked for less than ten seconds before finding the clearly labeled originals. He pulled them off the shelf and opened the folder.

Easy as that. The good stuff wasn't even taped down. He slid them into his container, put the forgeries in their place, opened the door, looked both ways, and stepped down the hall and out into the cool night air. He walked briskly for two blocks, taking deep breaths of the ocean air. He had left New York six months earlier—just ahead of the drug dealer who wanted his money or else—and now he wondered why he had waited so long to move west. Everything was easy here. He still used drugs, but he no longer sold them. He did very well prowling around the homes of the well-to-do.

Venice, with its stagnated canals and popular drug culture, was also one of—there seemed to be more than one of everything in Los Angeles—the city's artist hangouts and gallery centers. He turned west and walked the short block to the cement sidewalk bordering the beach. He stepped into a doorway immediately adjacent to a large, virtually abandoned public parking lot. He waited in the shadows, his folder pressed against the door.

Within minutes he saw the headlights bounce over the speed-control bump at the entrance to the lot. The car paused, then pulled up immediately opposite the doorway where he waited.

"Well?" He made the *w* sound almost like a *v*, but not quite enough to sound like a parody of a German accent.

"Fine. Fine. I just don't like working with people around me. Too risky."

"You won't have to do it again."

Then came the dog and bit the cat. He was knocked unconscious as he slid the forgeries into the backseat of the car. His last thought was of the little Avis sticker in the rear window. He was driven across the large lot to a dark spot right on the edge of the beach. There, he was dragged into the open, empty men's toilet. His sport coat was pulled roughly from him, and his shirt nearly torn off. A fatal dose of heroin was injected into his arm.

His body was discovered by a wino the next morning. It took the police a week to identify the body and to assemble his record. No one claimed his body, which was eventually cremated. His death—listed officially as an accidental overdose—disappeared into a computer bank, as completely as he himself had ceased to exist.

"IS THAT the only time you've been shot at?" Rachel was looking at the small scar on Jeffrey's arm near his shoulder.

"Isn't once enough? And you waited all this time to ask?" He was wrapped in a towel, his face covered with lather. There was a small drop of blood on his chin where he had cut himself.

"Since you've been full of surprises since I met you, I thought I'd save my question for a while."

"I see." He yanked a tissue from the box and dabbed the cut.

"Well?"

He turned and looked at her. She was in her robe, carefully applying her makeup, typically meticulous. Her assurance, and her beauty, momentarily distracted him from her question.

"Well?"

"It's the only time I've been hit."

"That's only part of the answer. Besides, I know all

about that," she said, gently touching the scar. "I meant
shot at, not hit. I know you've only been wounded once.
I looked."

"OK. When I was covering the landing of the marines
in Santo Domingo. Nineteen sixty-six, I think."

"And?"

"A big gas company, Exxon I think it was, had plas-
tered half of the United States with billboards showing an
aggressive tiger. Their slogan was 'Put a Tiger in Your
Tank.' So there I was in Santo Domingo, in a slum near
the airport. The garbagemen had been on strike for three
weeks and the place stank. I was walking along the edge
of a hill, trying to get a story together before curfew, and
I came across the billboard. Only it said *'Ponga un Tigre
en Su Tanque,'* or something like that. I stood there looking at it, struck by the irony that in the middle of squalor
and a revolution, commerce, as usual, dominated."

He paused.

"Jeffrey, the deal is when you agree to answer a question, you answer it."

He smiled at her. "I was standing there, looking at the
billboard, and I heard two shots. I turned to see where
they came from, intending to check out what was going
on. I had the conceit of everyman: It never occurred to
me anyone would shoot at me. When the third shot hit
the billboard just above my head, I realized they were
aiming at me."

He loved to tease her, so he stopped again, giving his
undivided attention to dabbing his cut.

"Dammit, Jeffrey, tell the story." She was trying—
none too successfully—to hide a smile. What didn't escape her lips came right out of her eyes.

"I dove down the side of the hill and stayed as close to
the ground as I could. I waited a few minutes and was
just about to get up when the whole goddamned billboard blew up. They'd hit it with a mortar."

"They who?"

"Either the government forces or the rebels. I never found out which."

"What did you do?"

"Same thing everybody else does at times like that."

"Which is?"

"I squeezed my butt real tight because I was afraid I was going to shit my pants."

She wrinkled her nose in disgust and frowned.

"No, really. That's what happens. I waited until I thought I had control of myself, then rolled down the rest of the hill and scrambled between buildings until I found a highway. A U.S. Marine patrol eventually picked me up and took me back to my hotel."

Rachel put the finishing touches on her makeup as Jeffrey stepped into the bedroom and began dressing. It was a typical weekday morning. He had gone out for a run and she had rushed off for an exercise class. As usual, they had arrived back home at almost the same time, both in a hurry to shower and get to work. Jeffrey showered in the bathroom next to one of their extra bedrooms, a room hung with posters and cluttered with the teenage paraphernalia for his son, Michael, during his weekend and frequent weekday visits.

"Henry's coming by to help hang the show. How about you?" she asked, as he pulled on his sport coat and disentangled his shirt cuffs.

"What time?"

"Lunch. About twelve-thirty. And if we don't get done before dinner, I've asked him to eat with us."

"I'll be there."

Henry Thurmond, self-proclaimed aging aesthete, had come into their lives when Rachel had offered one of the Grosz drawings to the Los Angeles County Museum. He was a curator on the museum's staff, an expert on twentieth-century American art. Henry was educated, elegant, and witty, and the three had become good friends. Henry lived alone in a house in the Hollywood Hills he had rebuilt himself with his customary good taste. They were all approximately the same age, which, Henry had observed, was somewhere between thirty-seven and death. He was a serious scholar, omnivorous reader, and tireless worker. His work was his life, and like many single people, his work was his closest friend as well. He was, Rachel and Jeffrey assumed, gay. They wished he had someone in his life, and had often asked him to bring a friend along to dinner. It had never happened.

Henry supplemented his curator's income with appraisals, taking wise advantage of the network of experts available to him. He had appraised Lena Sabin's Grosz collection at $476,000. The paintings, he had diplomatically said, were not prime Grosz and had they been they would have been worth much, much more. The drawings were very good, but sold for less than the paintings. Rachel had asked his advice about which drawing to donate to the museum, and Henry, with typical finesse, had chosen three but left the final decision to Rachel.

He had been fascinated by Jeffrey's rare-book business and full of questions about it. When all the appraising had been done and the friendship formed, they had presented Henry with a signed book of Matisse drawings from the artist's later years. Matisse was a particular idol of Henry's, and the book had become one of his most treasured possessions.

By eleven that morning Jeffrey was upstairs in his office cursing at his computer and his catalog and returning phone calls. Rachel, considerably more serene, was in her gallery, waiting for the framer to deliver her art. They both heard the truck pull up. Jeffrey suppressed his desire to watch the unloading. Rachel looked up and grinned at

Deborah Carlson, her one employee. Deborah was a
USC fine-arts graduate with the sunny disposition of a
born salesperson and the knowledge to back it up. Woe
betide anyone who called her Debbie. She stood by the
door, clipboard in hand, checking off the inventory as the
art was carried off the truck. That done, she scurried
across the brick walkway outside the gallery to a neigh-
boring restaurant to pick up the four spinach salads
Rachel had ordered.

Moments later Rachel heard Jeffrey thumping down
the stairs from his office. He rushed in, looked about, and
said, "Where's Henry?"

"Not here yet. But look what is here." She swung her
arm around to sweep the room and the art stacked carefully against the walls. "Let's start unwrapping."

She took off her sweater, handing it to Jeffrey as he
removed his coat. They were a well-matched couple and
they knew it. They were attractive and reasonably stylish. She had rich black hair and deep blue eyes that she
accented with makeup, a sensual mouth, and a trim figure she worked hard to maintain. They both liked to eat,
and they both could cook. He, no matter what he ate,
remained in good shape, which he credited to running.
His hair was light brown or blond, depending on the impact of the Southern California summer sun, and he had
begun to gray slightly. Like most bookish people, he
wore glasses, and had begun to fret as he realized bifocals
would perch on his straight nose before long. He tanned
easily; a good run even in winter would color him. She,
however, had milky-white skin and burned easily. That
summer, when they had bought their house, she had
taken a short nude sunbath and had emerged with bright
red burns on her buttocks. Jeffrey, with high good
humor, had insisted on applying lotion to her burns frequently. Thereafter, when they lay nude by their pool on

weekends, Rachel stayed under an umbrella. Jeffrey, to her consternation, got darker and darker. All over.

They were on their knees unwrapping the art when Henry arrived, followed seconds later by a salad-laden Deborah. All four immediately set to work.

"Perfect, absolutely perfect," Henry said, inspecting the frames. "Neutral and plain. Let the work show itself. No ornamentation."

"At the time he did them, were frames like this?" Jeffrey asked.

"Nope. More ornamental," Henry replied as Rachel nodded in confirmation. "Bauhaus was having its impact, but not yet on something like framing. The less-is-more philosophy hadn't taken hold yet."

Henry was the only one among them wearing a suit and tie. He had opened his collar, removed his coat, and rolled up his sleeves to go to work. He amused them by reporting on his morning with one of the museum's many committees of ambitious ladies. He was happy to be rid of them.

It took nearly five hours to get all fourteen works hung, a process complicated by Rachel and Henry's frequent indecision about which picture was to go where. Each time they changed their minds Jeffrey pulled hooks from the newly painted walls and patched the holes with spackle, which now spotted the front of his shirt.

They were standing back and admiring their work when Mike, fourteen years old and the possessor of an endless supply of energy, bounded into the gallery. He had little taste or time for art that wasn't, as he once put it, rock 'n' roll. He had his mother's good looks, his father's disposition, and the unqualified love of them both, plus Rachel's affection as well.

"What do you think, Mike?" Rachel asked after he had looked at the art and could no longer conceal his consternation.

"Interesting," he said diplomatically. His audience laughed.

"What's so funny?"

"That's what people say when they don't know quite what to say about art," Rachel explained.

Mike was nothing if not candid. "Oh, I know what to say. That's why I said 'interesting' instead."

"We're cooking pasta tonight. Want to come home with us?" his father asked.

"Can't. I told Mom I'd be home for dinner and I've got a ton of homework."

"You can have a swim," Rachel offered.

"This weekend. And you promised we'd all go to a movie."

"Right," Rachel agreed without consulting Jeffrey. The truth, though she wasn't about to admit it, was that she liked to be included in their father-and-son outings.

"So, Lena's taste in art sucks," Jeffrey commented as he watched Mike unlock his bicycle and ride off. "I hope the other critics don't say that."

They were struck by the beauty, passion, and frequent anger in Grosz's work, which, on the walls in their plain white frames, seemed all the more forceful. The three paintings were richly colored. One was a simple portrait of a woman in a coat who seemed prim and plain in comparison to the other two paintings, which were of prostitutes. In one, the woman had unselfconsciously spread her legs and was about to fondle one of her large, exposed breasts. The other, the one Jeffrey and Rachel had chosen to keep, was also nude, her pubic hair matching the dark color of her stockings, the smile of her lips welcoming and uninhibited.

The drawings were much smaller, though they made a much more forceful statement. Limbs were missing from some of the men, shattered veterans of Germany's obsession with war. In others, the businessmen, the generals, the politicians, missing limbs were replaced with weapons or industrial materials. They were grotesque, and so were their fat, complacent bourgeois women, fiddling with their pearls and primping before their pocket mirrors.

Small wonder Hitler, when he came to power, loathed the work of Grosz. It was said that when the Führer sent his thugs after Grosz, the artist himself had answered the door. He was dressed in his painting clothes, smudged and dirty. He convinced his armed enemies he was nothing more than the janitor and that the artist had fled. The story might have been apocryphal, but Grosz soon fled Germany. He emigrated to the United States and continued to torment the dictator with his drawings.

"Well, my friends," Henry said, rubbing his hands in anticipation, "two days until show time."

□□□ 7 ■

THEY WERE both nervous, but when Henry arrived early, a sea of calm, they became less so.

"This is only the most important night of my career," Rachel remarked, half hoping there might still be another somewhere.

"Then enjoy it," Henry suggested. "You've done all the ground work, now you hustle the guests."

This is what she did, though tentatively at first and with only a small amount of confidence later as it became obvious the evening was a success. She had anticipated everything. The caterers, who were inventive and had never worked the jaded art-gallery crowds, were circulating, offering good wine, unusual hors d'oeuvres, and constantly replenishing their supplies upstairs in Jeffrey's kitchen. She had hired a valet-parking service, in part to take the edge off finding a place to park in the crowded neighborhood, and also to remove the stigma—real or imagined—of attending a gallery show in the valley. Foolish prejudices are the slowest to die.

She was wearing a well-cut green wool suit, a white silk blouse, her best pearls, with the small diamond-and-emerald clasp on a long gold chain Lena had left her. Jeffrey was fitted out in his best pinstripe suit, his collar starched and his rep tie brand new. Henry, as usual, was in a tailor-made British suit, a carefully muted Glen plaid that would have looked good in a gathering of potentates.

As promised, Henry stuck close by her, pointing out the prominent, the powerful, the moneyed, the doubtful, and the press as people began to arrive and the party assumed its own momentum. Henry circulated easily—this was his métier—and he did so without an ounce of cynicism. He cared for art, and he also cared for Jeffrey and Rachel. Whenever he found someone even remotely interested in the art he started talking, punctuating his words with both enthusiasm and knowledge.

At first Rachel and Jeffrey stood together, a united front against the onslaught. Within minutes, Henry had pried them apart and sent them on their way to conduct the conversations he had rehearsed with them earlier. Rachel found the ritual of mixing social and business talk easier than did Jeffrey, who was accustomed to detailed talk about book collecting. Soon, however, he too was shaking hands and smiling at strangers.

Within an hour, the gallery was packed. The art season was in full swing, and word of Rachel's show had spread among the cognoscenti.

"There are too many," she complained to Henry. "They won't be able to see the art."

"They will if they want," he told her. "Most of them are here to see each other anyway." She frowned, wishing it wasn't so but understanding. She struck up a conversation with the woman who headed one of the County Museum's important committees. She prayed she knew more about Grosz than the woman, who possessed what Rachel had come to think of as the California Power Look: lifted face, tucked tummy, expensive clothes, valuable jewelry, but none of it obscuring intelligence.

Jeffrey made the first sale, a drawing of a Weimar general whose empty head erupted with visions of machine guns and tanks while his plump hands fondled the ample behind of his mistress. Jeffrey had earlier spotted the names of three well-known book collectors on the guest list, and they, it turned out, were also art collectors. He made a point of greeting all three and talking individually to them. It worked: One of them bought.

"Try not to look too surprised," he whispered to Rachel less than an hour after the crowds arrived, "but the party's paid for." She didn't immediately understand, so he added, "I just sold that one over there, so I get to put the first red sticker on the list."

Rachel wanted to hug him, but instead she smiled, opened the drawer of the receptionist's desk, and pulled a small red dot off a piece of wax paper. Without raising her hands out of the drawer, she handed the dot to Jeffrey. He quickly scanned the inventory list in the drawer, and placed the little dot next to the sold drawing. Then he took a pen and wrote the buyer's name next to it, and underlined the price: $9,000. She patted his hand.

"I'll collect my commission later," he whispered as he walked away. She thought she could detect a slight swagger, one for her benefit only.

At Henry's suggestion, they tried whenever possible to position themselves in conversations so that they could see the entrance to the gallery and observe newcomers. Because he was on a first-name basis with most of what he called the heavy-money art crowd, Henry stayed closest to the door, intercepting the right people and bringing them to Rachel. To the uninitiated, the gathering may have seemed like nothing more than a crowd of well-dressed people milling about in groups or wandering off alone to gaze. Instead, a ritual of social choreography was under way, with four principal performers. The stars were on the wall for all to see. The three moving players danced in a pattern, briefly appearing before each group of people. Their audience on this occasion was most appreciative.

All three stayed in character, and only Rachel broke out of her role briefly once to hug two other gallery owners, one she had once worked for and another who had sent her some of her first customers. Her conversations with them were necessarily brief, something they understood all too well from their own shows.

Henry sipped wine, shook hands, and, for all his innate reserve, seemed to be the hail fellow well met. Jeffrey and Rachel drank only Perrier water, tried to look at ease, and prayed their smiles betrayed no anxiety. Rachel paused occasionally to take deep breaths and several times had to suppress the urge to walk outside the gallery to look into the window and imprint what she saw forever in her memory. Jeffrey paused too, but only long enough to wipe his perspiring palms on his handkerchief. The reception was scheduled to last three hours, and by the time the third hour had begun the crowd had started to thin out slightly. Rachel and Jeffrey began to relax.

Rachel was in the middle of the large room when she saw a well-tailored, tall blond man consult the small catalog and look up at a painting. He then looked directly at her.

"I'm Rachel Sabin. Can I answer any questions for you?" She extended her hand.

He took it. "Are you certain this drawing was made in 1915?" Above the noise of the crowd, his voice was hard to distinguish, but she thought she detected an accent.

"Quite certain. But I'd be happy to have it double-checked if you'd like."

"I should think a year, maybe two, earlier. Before the war started, perhaps?"

His accent was German. His question, his attempt at correction, was stated politely. She was meant not to take offense.

"Why do you say that?" He might, after all, be right.

"In his drawings after the war started, in particular after he himself was drafted into the army, usually contain a bit of blood, a slight wound, and in many of them you see in the background some hint of the horror of war. There is none of it here. He was a cynical man, but his background was of the proletariat and he had great concerns about humanity."

Rachel knew all of this, but made no attempt to show it. Instead, she tried to change the course of the conversation:

"I'm sorry, I didn't hear your name."

"Karl Diedrich. I'm a dealer, though primarily in contemporary art. I have a personal interest in Grosz and own a drawing myself."

"I'm not familiar with your gallery, Mr. Diedrich."

"No reason why you should be." He smiled, bowing slightly. "I'm from Berlin. I'm here on business and a friend mentioned your show. I hope you don't mind my coming without an invitation—my friend assured me it was acceptable."

"If you are an admirer of Grosz, then you should be here. I'm delighted you came."

He smiled at her, and extended his hand again—this time in thanks.

Less than an hour later, when fewer than a dozen people remained in the gallery, Rachel gave in to her urge. She stepped outside and looked in the window. Her imagination filled the room once again with people, and stored the image.

□□□ 8 ∎

BY THE following morning, five of the thirteen works had red dots by their sides, and there were holds on three more, including one of the paintings, the large oil portrait of the stern woman that formed such a startling contrast to the two other paintings of prostitutes. Rachel had thought it would be the one least likely to sell, for it had none of Grosz's uninhibited sexuality and little of his irony, though it was the best example of his painterly technique. It would take time. The hold was at the request of an oil-company executive who was president of one of the County Museum's support groups, an organization comprised of businessmen and known for its lavish gifts. She anticipated visits from several committees before the final decision was made, and she knew as well that the man could make a recommendation but that it was up to the museum director and his curator to make the final decision. She couldn't wait until they showed up.

Parties of the sort that had occurred the night before

usually mark an ending. Not so in the art world. They signify beginnings, in this case Rachel's attempt to take her place among the more seriously considered galleries in Los Angeles. Also, the exhibition of an established, if not formidable, artist such as Grosz would also serve to attract local artists to her fold.

There was much to do. She was at her desk early, making a list of the people she had met, sorting through the pile of business cards she had collected, taping them on larger cards and placing them in her Rolodex. On each card she made notes of her conversations with its owner, recording interests, position, and anything else that might help her in future dealings. She had, in one short evening, compiled an enviable list of potential clients and, in fact, had made appointments with several of them to come back the following week.

There was more. Henry, smooth as ever, had struck up a conversation with a couple who were active in the La Jolla Museum of Contemporary Art, and had discovered they were considering selling two David Hockney prints in their collection. Rachel, Jeffrey, and Henry had agreed weeks before: find the right Hockneys and they'd buy them together, share them for a while, then decide whether or not to sell them. Both, Henry had told her, were prime examples of Hockney's printmaking, and both dealt with his long infatuation with the colors and lifestyles of Southern California. His advice to his partners: Buy them even if the price is high.

Although she thought of herself as a shrewd bargainer, she was half tempted to call the couple and arrange the purchase on the phone. Henry had their word the prints were in fine condition. That, and she wanted them and she knew Jeffrey did too. Jeffrey's interest in art, his enthusiastic support for what she was doing, pleased her greatly. They had both enjoyed the reception—more in retrospect than in its course—and their lovemaking later that night confirmed it. She was remembering his touch and his taste, and feeling the warmth begin to spread inside her again, when the gallery door opened and the German man walked in. She blushed slightly, as if he could read her mind. She had forgotten his name. He had not left a card to help her remember.

"Hello again." She quickly flipped through the unfiled cards before her just to make certain his wasn't among them.

"Good morning, Miss Sabin. I gather it was a successful evening," he remarked, nodding at the red dots next to several of the drawings.

"Yes, it was. Thank you. I'm sorry, but I've forgotten your name."

"Karl Diedrich." Once again he extended his hand.

"I haven't had the date checked on the Grosz drawing yet, but a friend of mine tells me it was drawn in 1914, late in the year, just before war broke out." The words "broke out" struck her as peculiar, as if the war were a rash, not a catastrophe. "Before Germany started the war," she corrected herself.

"Ah yes. We have a history of starting things. No more, I think. Did you know it's a crime for any citizen of Berlin to carry a weapon? A capital offense, even if that weapon is only a butcher's knife."

"No, I didn't." She was amazed there could be such a law, and she couldn't wait to tell Jeffrey. He was always surprising her with odd bits of history; this time she could surprise him.

"Last night, after I left, I kept thinking about one of the drawings. That one," he said, walking across the room to look at a fat, slightly pompous tuxedoed man holding a glass, looking up the dress of a plump maid, who was bent over, placing a bottle of champagne into an ice bucket. The top of her stockings and the beginning of her fleshy buttocks were the focus of his intense gaze. *"Nach Tish,"* Diedrich said to her, smiling.

"After the meal," she translated. And it was obvious who was going to be dessert. The thought made her color slightly, especially since he was looking directly at her.

"May I ask the price?"

"Four thousand dollars." She could have made an offer of a 20 percent discount, as was custom with dealers doing business among themselves, but she decided not to. Let him ask for it.

"I'll take it."

He caught her completely by surprise. It was the easiest sale she had ever made.

"You're welcome to think it over, if you'd like. I'd be happy to put a hold on it."

"That won't be necessary. I'll leave you a check and pick it up at the end of the exhibit. When will that be?"

"Six weeks."

The address he gave her was in New York, though he claimed to spend little time there and maintained his apartment and an account in dollars at the Deutsche Bank's New York office so that checks he wrote in the United States could clear more quickly and he could avoid the pitfalls and delays of international banking.

"My apartment is small. Mostly storage space and a place for me to sleep," he added, smiling evenly. "I understand you deal quite a bit in contemporary art."

"Yes, I do. Californians mostly, but also prints and occasional paintings by other American artists."

"If you're not too busy, I'd very much like to see some of what you have."

For the next hour they looked at and talked about art.

She learned that he liked Hockney as much as she did, and he spoke knowledgeably about the German Neo-Expressionists. She showed him a painting by Frederick Wight, whose studies of light and motion, particularly as it was shaped by the California landscape, had at one time been plentiful, but had become less so when Wight died the year before. When he responded to the painting with interest, she pulled two more from her storage room. One seemed to keep his interest more than the others, a sentry palm bending in the hot wind called *Santa Ana Blowing*.

"Just when you think figurative painting has no future, you see something like this. He really is very good."

"Yes, he is. And undervalued. The art gallery at UCLA is named for him. He taught there many years. He was, for me, a precursor for all the things that are happening here now." Not sure he knew what she meant, she added, "The new museums, the Getty fortune."

"Competing with New York will not be so simple," he remarked.

"I really don't think of it as competing. We are adding to art, and while some may still think of it as regional, we out here don't agree."

"You might try convincing the art magazines of that," he said, still contemplating the Wight.

She nodded in agreement. If the art world was small and incestuous, the magazines that reported on that world were even more so, and provincial as well. It was a common complaint in the museum world and among the gallery owners, artists, and collectors. Obviously, the man knew what he was talking about.

"Frank Stella, for instance," he said as he leaned casually against the counter in her storage room. Casual seemed out of context for him. It was Saturday, yet he was wearing a coat and tie, a conspicuous deviation from the weekend norm in Los Angeles.

She nodded in agreement and he continued.

"He has an international reputation, and is extremely popular in Germany. He is noted for being an Eastern American artist, yet most of his early—and some would say his best—prints he made here in Los Angeles."

"At Gemini."

"Yes. I have one just now, a very good one. I just bought it from a client in Santa Barbara."

"Oh?" She hoped she hid her interest. Jeffrey had a particular passion for Stella's work. The big print from the *Had Gadya* in their living room was their prize possession. Stella's earlier works, especially those printed in California, were very rare. And usually very expensive.

"River of Ponds."

"You say you have it for sale? I might be interested." More than might. It was part of a series that showed Stella as a master of the form: precise, beautifully colored, and one of his dazzling geometric protractor series.

He had counted on her interest. "Yes, it is for sale. I have it here with me now, as a matter of fact. I was just about to take it to be crated and shipped to New York. Would you like to see it?"

She would. While he went to get it from his car, Rachel quickly telephoned Henry. Stella prices were not her strong suit, but they were one of Henry's. Luckily, he was in. Usually ebullient and chatty, Henry was strictly business when it came to money. He listened, then told her not to pay over $7,000 for it, and then only if it was in excellent condition. "If it's to be a bargain, then a bargain it should be. I don't remember meeting him. Remind him you can save him crating and shipping charges too."

She hurried into her office and looked among the reference books lined neatly on her shelves. She withdrew her copy of *The Prints of Frank Stella,* Richard Axsom's catalogue raisonné, then walked back into the gallery, book in hand.

He carried the wrapped print easily, his demeanor still somewhat formal. The only difference from when he had first walked in was that to grip the square frame his arms were extended and his brushed-gold cuff links were exposed. His tie and jacket remained perfectly in place. He held it out almost as an offering; his unstated question was where to put it. He was, she noted, impeccably well mannered and correct.

"Against the wall over there, if that's all right with you. Would you like something to drink? Tea, coffee? I think there's also some wine left over from last night."

"Tea, thank you. No sugar."

Before she looked at the print, she made tea for them both, passing over the usual mugs and placing each cup on its saucer. She tried to hide her excitement and hoped it didn't show.

It did, of course, and he had already noticed it. He was on his hands and knees, carefully wiping his thumbprints from the glass with a handkerchief.

She stood back, looked, and knew immediately she wanted it. But only if the price was right. She stepped closer, reading the signature, noting it was print number 68 of 70. She inspected the blind stamp. Then the print itself: It was a perfect impression. The colors were spectacular: geometric eclipses of soft coral, pink, gray, and turquoise. It had been printed in 1971. After examining it, she opened the print book and found it. Diedrich, seemingly accustomed to other dealers checking their references, smiled politely.

"How much are you asking for it, Mr. Diedrich?"

She could be formal too, but it didn't come as easily to
her as it did to him.

"Please call me Karl. I think five thousand dollars.
That is, if you like it and agree with the price."

"Oh, I like it." She liked the price even better.

"I can tell," he said, smiling.

"I'll write you a check."

"Then I think a professional discount would be in
order."

It was better than a bargain, and now he was offering
a discount. She hadn't even offered him one. "Thank
you. I'll also discount your Grosz."

Ten minutes later the paperwork was done. He had
Rachel's check, and she had his. They had exchanged addresses and telephone numbers. She had the Stella and, in
six weeks, he would have his Grosz.

"I think I might even know of some other Stella
prints," he said as he was leaving. "Would you be interested?"

"Most certainly." Stella's work was hard to come by,
carefully controlled by his galleries and vigorously sought
after by galleries and collectors alike. "Would you like me
to call you when the show is over, or will you be back?
We can also ship the print to you."

"I'm not certain just yet." He stepped to her desk and
added another telephone number to his New York address. He included the international code for direct-dial-
ing Berlin.

"Well, then. We've both accomplished a lot this
morning. I hope to see you soon."

They shook hands. After he was gone, she con-
templated the Stella, then buzzed Jeffrey upstairs to tell
him about it. He had left for lunch and so she called
Henry. He whistled at the price she had paid. It had been
better than a bargain.

□□□9∎

A HOT, dusty, and dry unseasonal Santa Ana wind seared Los Angeles, transforming February from a moist month into a tinderbox waiting for a small spark to explode. By nightfall the air was so clear and so dry, the lights of the city made it look as though someone had dumped a treasure chest of jewels about the landscape, then sent up a full moon to artfully illuminate them. While the rest of the country froze in the throes of winter, the citizens of Los Angeles mopped their brows, scratched their itchy skin, and blamed everything on the weather.

Wind brings its own peculiar hazard to this most synthetic of cities. The electricity it generates finds its way into carpeting, wallpaper, doorknobs, and anything else with shocking power. Anything that could retain the electrical energy stored it, only to discharge it whenever contact was made with the human body.

Rachel maneuvered around the peril by daintily flicking her fingers against any metal surface before she touched it, letting her nails absorb the shock. Jeffrey did

so as well, but with less success. He was helping out in
the kitchen when he accidentally pressed his groin against
the kitchen counter. The moment his body came into
contact with the narrow metal counter guard, he let out a
painful yelp.

It was a dangerous night to be a fireman, and it was a
delightful night for Jeffrey, Rachel, and Henry. They
were about to celebrate by dining outdoors beside the
pool. Jeffrey, like so many other men, was only mildly
useful in the kitchen, but adroit at a barbecue. Outdoors,
he could cook anything. Indoors, as Rachel put it, he
could—and did—burn everything. He had marinated the
chicken halves himself, and was about to put them on the
grill.

"Henry's late—you'd better wait," Rachel cautioned.

"Damn, the fire is perfect."

"You'd be a disaster working in a restaurant. People
don't like to eat only when the chef's ready." She was in
the kitchen, comfortably air-conditioned, the window
over the sink opened a crack so she could speak with
Jeffrey. She could see the shine of sweat on his forehead
as he leaned from the hot air into the hotter air of the
barbecue. When he heard Henry's car in the driveway he
hurried through the house to greet him. As he passed
through the living room he paused to look at the big
Stella on the wall, and the smaller, newer one propped on
the floor beside it. It filled him with a pleasurable sense of
wonder to realize this art was in their house.

"Shit," he yelped as he touched the doorknob and felt
the quick surge of static electricity. He even saw the
spark.

"The usual warm greeting," Henry responded. "I
stopped to change clothes. I was soaked with sweat. My
car needs Freon, and it's a furnace."

"So does mine. Want some help?"

"The prints are in my trunk. You take one, I'll take the other."

Rachel stood in the doorway as they brought them in. They were wrapped in padded cotton packing sheets Henry had borrowed from the museum. Earlier that afternoon he had driven south to La Jolla, a check for $14,000 from Rachel's gallery account in his wallet, to pick up the two Hockney prints they had agreed to buy. Henry and Rachel both knew them from their Hockney catalogs. Jeffrey had never seen them.

"Wait, wait. Don't unwrap them yet. Let's have a ceremony."

"I hope that means a drink, Rachel."

"It does." She hurried into the kitchen and reappeared moments later with a tray of freshly chopped vegetables, dip, three chilled glasses, and a cold bottle of wine. "Now!"

They all stood back as Henry pulled the prints out of their wrapping. It would be difficult to imagine two more sharply contrasting works by David Hockney. *Dark Mist,* one of his earlier California works, was printed in an edition of only twenty-five in 1973. It was of a building and three palm trees in a dense, coastal fog. The trees were nearly swallowed by the fog, and the print itself was dark and moody, black, white, and gray with none of Hockney's customary vibrant colors. It was absolutely still.

"Oh God, that's gorgeous," Jeffrey said. "I expect to see Ingrid Bergman and Humphrey Bogart walk through it any minute." Jeffrey loved it immediately, and Rachel made no attempt to hide her pleasure at his reaction.

The other print was *Afternoon Swimming,* awash with motion and alive with color, an azure-blue swimming pool beside a bright-green lawn, an orange inflatable raft bobbing in the water, with coral abstract swimmers splashing in the pool. There was movement, pleasure, and even luxury in looking at it. It was the newer of the two prints, struck in 1979.

"Makes you want to go swimming," Henry remarked.

"And that's what I intend to do as soon as we eat. You two have a tough decision to make. There's a friendship resting on it," Jeffrey commented. "Or ending over it."

"What about you?" Rachel asked.

"This isn't my deal," Jeffrey said, smiling. "You and Henry are the art partners here, not me. I'm a lowly bookdealer."

"But this is your house too," Henry countered, "and one of these prints is going to be on your wall for a year."

That was the deal. Henry and Rachel had bought them together, with the understanding they would each have one print for a year, then decide whether to sell them in her gallery. Though they had spent $14,000 for the two, the purchase was made as a dealer and was well below the market price. Given Hockney's soaring popularity, a year would add substantially to their value, possibly even double it.

Jeffrey shook his head at Henry's polite offer to weigh in on the decision. "Look out, Henry, Rachel always gets what she wants."

Neither Jeffrey nor Rachel had ever imagined that one day, along one wall of their living room, would hang a big Frank Stella, and sitting on the floor alongside it would be another, smaller Stella and two Hockneys. It was a moment to relish. They sat on the sofa and sipped their wine while Henry leaned against an arm of the sofa, smoking a cigarette. Several moments passed before Jeffrey broke the spell.

"Impossible choice, that's what it is. I pity you both."

"If I had to choose among all four prints, I know the one I don't want," Henry said.

"Which is that?" Rachel asked, looking directly at him, hoping the decision was already made.

"The big Stella from the *Had Gadya* series."

"Why?"

"Too Jewish."

Rachel laughed. "Maybe it helps if you know the story."

An hour later, Jeffrey's perfectly cooked chicken was little more than picked bones. The rice was gone and the salad bowl empty. Only the wine remained, and beads of sweat were warming it in the hot night air. A candle flickered in the center of the table, anticipating the wind that would blast again the next day.

"Well, it's coming up on decision time." Rachel and Henry had both declined to state their choice, and Jeffrey liked to tease.

"What is the story behind the *Had Gadya?*" Henry, like many in his profession, sought information about everything.

"It's a parable," Rachel said, linking her fingers and resting her chin on them. "Very much like 'The Twelve Days of Christmas.'"

"A song I would be grateful never to hear again," Jeffrey added.

Henry nodded in agreement. He took off his steel frame glasses, rubbed his eyes, and looked at Rachel. "Go on—it's story time."

"Children recite it at Passover. It's part of the holiday ritual. It begins with a kid—a baby goat—who is devoured by a cat, which in turn is devoured by a dog, and on and on. Ours is *The Butcher Came and Slew the Ox.*"

"That must be pretty far into the parable. What's the point of the whole parable, the story?"

"The exodus of the Jews from Egypt."

"I'm just a Gentile who's going swimming. You two can discuss religious theories."

"Henry, you swim too. I'll clean up. Maybe a swim will sober Jeffrey up a little."

"I didn't bring a swimsuit."

"You don't need one," Jeffrey told him. "But look out—Rachel will sneak a look out of the kitchen window."

"Big deal," she said, picking up the empty plates.

"Might be," Jeffrey suggested.

He dove in first. The water was cool and restorative, sobering as well.

"Clears your head," Henry said, pushing his long black hair out of his face, "and I think I need a haircut." His conversation was uncharacteristically stilted, almost forced. Jeffrey wondered if Henry was uncomfortable swimming naked with him. He hoped not. It was, after all, practically a California convention. Both he and Rachel had decided that beneath Henry's charm and enthusiasm was a lonely man, and Rachel in particular worried about him from time to time. Jeffrey worried about him too, but unlike Rachel, he was not so quick to state his concerns. Among their small circle of mutual friends, Henry was the most cherished.

He had also assumed the role of Rachel's adviser, helping her choose art and using his museum connections to direct her purchases. Rachel had offered several times to pay him for his advice, but he had refused, carefully citing a potential conflict of interest. However, they had decided that one day they might become partners in an even larger gallery. Henry was tiring of the museum work, the low pay compensated by the elevated status among the art community. "Elevated," he once remarked, "means that your mind and your contacts have value, but your money is worthless."

Afternoon Swimming may have been Hockney's artistic preference, but night swimming was Jeffrey's. It was almost a form of collusion between the hot night air and the cool water, and it seemed to him it was one of the most relaxing things in the world. In the summer, he swam every night before going to bed. It wasn't exercise, it was luxury, and when he swam, almost always underwater, it felt as though he could hold his breath forever.

Henry was drying off and about to dress when Jeffrey emerged, wrapped himself in a big towel, and sat down. "Well, what's it going to be? *Afternoon Swimming* or *Dark Mist?*"

"I think you might be surprised," Henry said, smiling.

He was, and so was Rachel. Henry proposed they keep both Hockney prints, and that he take the smaller Stella, the *River of Ponds* that Rachel had just bought from Karl Diedrich.

"I like it best for several reasons," Henry explained. "One, I love its precision, its geometric perfection, and its formality. Two, the colors. Stella usually uses strong colors, but these are soft and, to me, more expressive. If it's OK with you."

It seemed to Rachel the offer was also one of friendship, the willingness to make a decision based on what might please the other, rather than himself. She looked to Jeffrey, who smiled at her as though he shared her thought. Then she agreed, sealing the pact by giving Henry a hug.

"I'll be damned," Jeffrey said at last. "I was looking forward to an agonized decision between the two of you."

□□□ 10 ∎

HE DROVE the van up the steep incline leading to Nob Hill, and as he did he nervously ground out a cigarette in the overflowing ashtray. San Francisco, as usual, was magnificently lit and he could see the tower of the Mark Hopkins hotel indignantly poking into a thick cloud bank, as though it were offended by any cloud that might spoil its dominance of the hilltop. He turned right into an alley just off Union Square. He had rehearsed it three times before and knew exactly where the building was and how to squeeze into the narrow loading dock.

His clipboard in hand, he jumped out and walked up to the night watchman, who was sitting on a tattered chair, picking at the remains of a soggy tuna sandwich.

"Markham Gallery. I'm expected."

"You sure somebody's up there?"

He could smell the liquor on the guard's breath. "I called ahead. They're expecting me."

Jesus, it was easy. He had said it would be, and had proceeded to outline exactly how it was to be done. The guard was lazy and usually half loaded by ten every night, and if there was any trouble, he was to shrug his shoulders and say if the delivery didn't get made it would be the guard's ass getting kicked. As it was, the guard didn't even resist. Easy money: $2,500 to exchange four big fake Frank Stella prints for the originals.

The man with the slight German accent had approached him in a popular gay bar in the Castro district. He was at his usual job, tending bar, and the German had struck up a conversation. At first he had thought the man was coming on to him, and for a while that was it. Then, later that night, as he was checking up the glasses from the final call, he had proposed they go for coffee. The conversation had been friendly and easy, and the German had encouraged him to talk about himself, about his day job working in an art gallery, his frustration with his high qualifications and his low pay. Then the German had made his proposition. His reservations had slipped away. He needed the money, needed it bad, and the whole thing sounded, well, like an adventure. He liked excitement almost as much as he liked money.

The key he had been given fit the lock and the magnetized metal strip he had been told would lock the alarm-system circuit slipped into the doorjamb exactly as he'd been told it would. It took less than three minutes—he was checking his digital watch from the time he put the key in the door—to exchange the prints and secure the originals in the flat packing box. They weren't even taped down. He smiled as he made the switch. Easy money.

As he turned to leave he saw a shaft of light from the streetlamp outside illuminating a corner of the gallery showroom. He squinted, but could not clearly see the two small statues on a pedestal in a corner. He flipped on the light switch, looked again, and muttered, "Be still my heart."

There, before him, were two magnificent Giacometti statues, no more than nine inches tall. To some they were silly little stick figures; to others, himself included, they were breathtaking works of art. These two were men, long in the leg, their chests brave and masculine. He stepped closer and could see their genitals distending between their legs. On an impulse, he grabbed them both and slid them inside his windbreaker. He could double his money—no, more—by selling one and he would keep the other.

The guard was tilted back on his chair and opened his eyes long enough to nod in the man's direction as he hoisted the box into the back of the van and went around to the driver's side. He jumped into the van, pulled the statues out of his jacket, and sat them on the seat beside him. He decided he would call them Bert and Ernie. There was still a lump in one of his jacket pockets. He reached in and found the gloves—which he had been told to wear—still unused.

He drove quickly back to the Castro and his small apartment. He had less than an hour until the German— he had given his name as Hans Greber—would be there to give him his money.

He poured himself a tumblerful of Scotch, then swallowed a couple of Quaaludes to calm himself down. He had been sweating, and so he pulled off his clothes and took a shower. He wanted to be clean, because he hoped that with the money would come sex with the attractive man. He pulled on sweat pants and a sweat shirt, then remembered to hide the statues. At first he couldn't figure out where. Finally he stuck them under his kitchen sink behind the cleansers and the big bag of cat food.

Just over half an hour had passed since he had arrived back at his apartment. He was about to take his first swallow of his third Scotch when the buzzer from the front door downstairs rang. He watched as the man climbed the stairs and stepped into his apartment.

"Did it go well?"

"Exactly as you said. The prints are in the van. It's parked just around the corner." He pointed in that direction.

"The keys?"

"There. On the table by the door. Would you like a drink?"

"Yes, thank you. Scotch." He smiled, removed his coat, and loosened his tie.

He was pouring the drink when he felt the German's hand reach around him, slide up under his sweat shirt, and caress the hair on his stomach. He smiled and leaned back as his sweat shirt slid up across his chest. He pulled it off, then reached for the drink he had poured.

Things were going very well indeed. As he turned to face the German he felt the man's hands untie his sweat pants and pull them down around his ankles. He was getting hard already. The last thing he saw as he turned was the German, smiling at him, his coat cloaking his hands, as he reached for his throat to strangle him.

His body was found the next day. He was nude, sprawled across his bed, and it took no time at all for the police to speculate what had happened. His stereo, his money, and all of his credit cards were missing. Obviously, he had picked up another man—probably in the bar where he worked. The wrong man. It happened all the time.

The missing Giacometti statues were reported the next morning by the owner of Markham Gallery, who was able to provide detailed descriptions of the statues as well as photographs of them. The owner was a shrewd and well-connected woman who was puzzled because so little had been stolen from a gallery that had a small fortune in artwork on its shelves and walls.

In less than a week, what at first appeared to be a routine murder began to be a deepening mystery. The statues had been discovered under the dead man's kitchen sink. It did not require a trained eye to know they were valuable: The police lieutenant who found them assumed they were simply because of where they were discovered.

The murdered man was named Alan Kinsolving. The coroner's routine autopsy report said there was semen in his rectum. The detectives who had examined the gallery had done an unusually thorough job. Kinsolving's fingerprints were found on the pedestal that had contained the statues, and also on a small partition in the gallery's art-storage bins that contained a new group of Stella prints. Then, the detective charged with bringing the dead man alive, at least on paper, learned Alan Kinsolving had a bachelor of arts and a master's degree in fine art from the Art Institute of Chicago.

An art restorer and expert in forgery from the De Young Museum was called in to examine the Stella prints. It took him less than two weeks to determine they were forgeries. Very good forgeries. He was also able to tell from the paper stock and from the print technique that the forgeries were probably made in Europe, possibly Germany, where sophisticated machinery and inks were manufactured.

The San Francisco newspapers, which, like newspapers anywhere, love a good murder, reported every detail. The police department communicated all the information they had to the Interpol headquarters in Europe, and—as was customary in cases involving art theft—to the International Foundation for Art Research in New York.

□□□ 11 ■

JEFFREY WONDERED at the endless idiosyncrasies of the people whose passion was collecting books. He was at his desk, waging a war endemic to his business and one he was incapable of winning. For every book there was a piece of paper. For every potential collector there were more pieces of paper. Keeping what seemed to him to be a self-contained ecological disaster area under control was impossible. He was sorting, making small piles, transferring what he could onto his word-processor file of customer want lists, struggling to keep his usually pristine desk uncluttered.

One man had written looking for a first edition of *Alcoholics Anonymous,* explaining he had been a member of the organization for nearly twenty years and, as a collector, wanted to buy a copy for his twentieth AA birthday. He would, if necessary, settle for a copy without a dust jacket. It was a request Jeffrey particularly wanted to honor, and he had spent considerable time trying to find a copy. He had written the names of fifteen dealers on the man's letter. He had called them all and not one had a copy or knew where to find one. The book, it turned out, was improbably rare, given AA's huge membership. The organization's founders, on a budget and vastly underestimating the potential impact of their work, had printed only some one thousand books. All but the first edition had been blue; thus the book had become known as the Big Book or the Blue Book. The first edition, however, was bright red, with a brightly colored dustcover. Copies in relatively good condition, with their jackets intact, printed in 1939, were now selling for $3,500. If one could be found.

Jeffrey doubted he would be able to find a copy in time for the man's anniversary, and had telephoned him in Omaha to tell him so. The next letter on the pile promised to be easier, and it amused Jeffrey to speculate about it. A man in Columbus, Ohio, had seen a copy of one of Jeffrey's catalogs and had written to say he collected books about nudists. He was looking for a mystery book he had heard of called *Murder Among the Nudists*. Jeffrey's research revealed there was such a book, published in 1934 and written by someone named Peter Hunt. It had taken half a dozen calls, but he had found it, bought it for $18, and was reselling it for $45.

He examined the book itself, and smiled. It had a green dust jacket with an actual photograph—genitals, pubic hair, and nipples all carefully airbrushed—of men and women frolicking in the buff, much like those the old nudist magazines used to publish. And, to add to the temptation, there was a tiny photo of nudes on the spine.

He addressed a label and put the book on a pile of others waiting to be wrapped and mailed. Jeffrey had a vision of the man's paneled study, its stately nature contrasting sharply with a couple very similar to that in

Grant Wood's *American Gothic* sitting, happily nude, contemplating their collection.

Another collector, far more serious and potentially a valuable customer, had reported in searching for P. G. Wodehouse's *By the Way Book*. Wodehouse had, in the years since his death in 1975, become increasingly popular among collectors. The great humorist's works had always been in demand, but now there was a bull market in his humor, something that no doubt would have provided great fodder for the satirical genius. The *By the Way Book* was one of his earliest to be published. It was known as *The Globe By the Way Book* and had been printed in 1908 by the London *Globe* newspaper. It was little more than a flimsy paperback, and no one was certain how many copies had originally been printed. But it was known that no more than twenty remained in existence and those few collectors fortunate enough to locate one paid $5,000 and up, depending on the condition of the book itself. It was quite unlikely Jeffrey could find a copy—he did not remember having seen one for sale in at least a decade. But he was willing to try. It was his willingness, his determination, and his knowledge that had made him a success, and time had not changed him at all.

He looked from his desk, which was now relatively neat, down to the floor beside it. Two piles of motion-picture scripts sat on the carpet, the corners of their title pages curled by time and storage. He had bought them from a retired studio script supervisor who had wisely assumed B movies in the 1930s and early 1940s might have value in the future. There, on the floor, waiting to be cataloged, were some of the earliest works of novelists imported to Hollywood by the studios, writers who had been forced to their typewriters by tyrannical studio heads, used, often abused, then dispatched far richer in both money and indignation than when they had arrived. Jeffrey groaned as he squatted on the floor to begin sorting through them, dividing two stacks into a series of smaller stacks that he would then catalog. As he looked at their titles and moved them about, he could hear conversations from Rachel's gallery on the floor below. He stopped, listened, and smiled.

Rachel was enduring one of the perils of her profession, and she had been dreading it for days. It was, she had said, a significant ritual, one that would be repeated rather often if she was successful, but nevertheless one she did not like. It involved what she had decided to call nouveau riche oblige, and at this moment she was surrounded by money: The museum support group that had placed a hold on one of the George Grosz paintings had dispatched its emissaries to her gallery to inspect the prize so they might dip into their abundant bank accounts.

"It was painted during his Berlin years," Rachel told the small gathering. "More precisely in 1927. The title, *Frau in Schwarzem Mantel,* translates as *Standing Woman in Black Coat.* It is a perfect portrait of a woman of those times, rather severe, dark, and an outstanding example of his nonsatirical work."

Rachel noticed one man and one woman in the group had looked away from the stern-faced *Frau* and were looking—she thought enviously—at the painting of the nude with black stockings idly applying her makeup. The man was concentrating on her mound of lush pubic hair; the woman focused on her nipples. The better of the two paintings, perhaps, but not for sale. She directed them back to the object of their visit with a brief sociological discussion of Berlin in the twenties, managing to mix repression and depression—which the painting seemed to her to symbolize—with the freewheeling, uninhibited nightlife of the city itself.

In all, there were six people who had come to the gallery for an hour or two of convincing.

"Given the number of paintings Grosz did during his career," Rachel continued, "there are relatively few of this sort, and nearly all are in museum collections and will not reappear in the marketplace."

Rachel noticed one of the women shift her Gucci shoulder bag from one arm to the other, idly adjust the big diamond ring on her finger, and then step gingerly out of one of her Chanel shoes. She had a bunion pad on one of her toes. The woman would have made a perfect satirical subject for Grosz. Rachel hid her smile. Then she mentally chastised herself: *These are good people who are customers. Think of them what you'd like, you need them for your business. They might, most of them, be pretentious and out of their depth, but it is your job to reassure them and to convince them they are doing the right thing.*

"Could I offer you some coffee or tea? Or perhaps something cold?"

She had few takers. It was getting too close to lunch, and they no doubt had plans. She knew that this committee would make its recommendation, only to be supplanted by another. They, in turn, would make their recommendation, and then the check would be issued. Though they thought of their decisions as recommendations, in fact they were not. The decision to acquire a piece of art was made by the museum director and his curators. Then the buck—literally and figuratively—was passed to a committee and on it went until the right committee—with the right amount of eagerness to please and the right amount of money—took over. Rachel, at Henry's suggestion, was asking $50,000 for the work. These were not the sort of people who quibbled about prices; it wasn't the custom. Still, she wondered if scholarship and commerce could ever mix effectively. She knew, at least on this particular day, that she wasn't paying as close attention to her guests as she pretended. Everything distracted her, including the telephone. Although her answering machine was picking up the calls, she nevertheless cocked an ear each time it rang. One voice she readily identified: Henry.

She wondered, shifting her weight to the other foot and issuing a perfunctory smile at one of the committee who was now looking at her, if the heat would ever end. She knew it would; it always did. But once the Santa Ana was blowing, it seemed as though it would go on forever. Her air conditioning was barely making it, and she had opened her back door for more air. Her patience was evaporating in the hot dry air, and she was running out of things to say.

It was after 5 P.M. before her day ended, and Rachel was convinced she had said all the right things to her visitors. She also knew, courtesy of Henry, that the oil-company executive who headed the support group did not like to have his "suggestions" overruled. The last time his group had done so, the executive himself, in a fit of pique, had bought the art in question for his own collection. The process of selection, she thought, was even less democratic than it appeared. That, somehow, was appropriate: You can't be democratic about art, no more than it is possible to dictate what is good and what is bad art. Hitler's determination to do just that had inspired Grosz to even greater heights of invention.

She checked her phone machine for the messages. One was from the painter who came in to repaint the walls before each new show, the second was from Henry.

"It's Henry. I've got a terrific idea for the Stella. Better than that I think I know where to get another one. I need to talk to you. I'll be at the museum this afternoon and home later tonight." He sounded rushed and, Rachel thought, a bit confused. She dialed his office, but he had already left. She erased the messages, tidied up the gallery, set the burglar alarm, and left. Jeffrey had already gone; his parking place was empty.

THEY HAD gone to Hollywood to see a movie and then out to dinner, making it, for them, a late night. Consequently, they overslept the next morning and missed their early exercise. As Rachel unlocked her gallery door, she was still sleepy and trying without much success to focus her attention on the new day. She had been unable to reach Henry the night before and as she opened the door she was thinking of him. She stepped to the small numbered panel to punch in her alarm code and stop the warning buzzer that always went off the instant she opened the door. She had punched in two of the four digits before she realized the buzzer was silent.

She punched in the code again, and as she did she realized the warning light was already green, the system already shut down. She was not an easily frightened woman, so instead of leaving the gallery and summoning Jeffrey from upstairs, she strode into the exhibit space, flipping on light switches as she went. Nothing was missing. She stepped into the small anteroom where the filing cabinets and coffee machine were, and from there to the doors of her office and her art-storage space. She closed and locked them both each evening as she left, and now they were open. Nothing appeared to have been touched and, from her initial inspection, nothing appeared to be missing. It was as disorienting as it was frightening. Her gallery had been broken into, but it did not seem to have been robbed. She reached for the phone and pushed the intercom buzzer to Jeffrey's office upstairs. She quickly told him what had happened and just as quickly heard him pounding down the stairs.

"Are you sure nothing is missing?"

"No, I'm not sure. It just doesn't look like it. Nothing has even been moved that I can tell. But everything's been unlocked."

"I'll call the police." He called, stated what had happened, listened, then said, "No, it is not in progress," paused for a second, and said, "I see." He did not say thank-you.

"They'll have someone here as soon as they can. I guess they figure there's no rush because there's no robbery under way and no one to catch."

"What do we do now?" Her initial fear was turning to anger.

"Look to see if anything is missing."

For the better part of an hour they looked through the gallery, Rachel with a typewritten copy of her inventory in her hand, methodically checking off each work of art as she found it. Jeffrey looked through drawers and filing cabinets, and then joined her, calling off the name of each work as he slid it out of the storage space.

He was attempting to reset the alarm system when a police officer walked in. His visit was brief and, for him as well as for Rachel and Jeffrey, confusing. Nothing was missing, and they had to convince the cop that the alarm had been in working order and that the gallery had actually been broken into.

"Maybe the alarm broke," he suggested.

"If it did, then how come two doors are unlocked and open? And my files open?" Rachel countered, her hands on her hips, her mood defiant.

The cop merely shrugged and made out his report, and in less than an hour concluded his visit by telling them they'd been lucky. Most of the stores he visited under similar circumstances, he said, had been thoroughly cleaned out. He didn't add what he was thinking: *Why would anyone want this stuff anyway?*

"Well?" Rachel turned to Jeffrey as soon as the cop left.

"I think you'd better call the alarm company and get them out here."

She thumbed her Rolodex quickly, paused, and, uncharacteristically, cursed.

"Shit. The number is at home with the papers. I did what you told me, but I forgot to write down the phone number here."

"I'll go and get it."

"It's in the last file in your desk drawer."

She set about checking her files and inventory once again, and Jeffrey left, only to reappear seconds later grinning sheepishly.

"My car keys are upstairs. Can I borrow yours?"

She couldn't resist a smile. Jeffrey and car keys were natural opposites: always in different places. She had put up a key rack by the back door, where the keys could always be found. Jeffrey's were seldom there, and Jeffrey's searches for them were vociferous and vindictive.

She was still checking her art against her inventory several minutes later when the phone rang.

"Somebody's been here too."

At first she didn't understand. Jeffrey continued:

"Every closet has been opened, and some furniture has been moved. But I can't find anything missing. I'm going to call the police."

"They're going to think we're nuts."

"I might agree with them."

Deborah was at the dentist and Rachel was alone in the gallery, still checking, trying all the time to apply some sort of logic to what was happening, when the door opened and a customer walked in. She looked up and saw, smiling easily at her, Karl Diedrich.

"Hello. I thought you'd gone to New York."

"I intended to, but something came up and I stayed an extra few days. And, since I was nearby, I thought I'd come by and look at my Grosz drawing once again."

He walked across the gallery and examined it, his hands clasped behind his back. Rachel noticed he was, as usual, well dressed and sure of himself.

"You were right about the date of the drawing. It was done after the war began. And your date of 1915 is correct. I called a Grosz expert who is a friend of mine in Germany. He confirms what you said. I was almost certain it predated the war."

Rachel, even in times of stress, could be courteous:

"I understand your question, though. To look at it and see the relative absence of carnage, one might think it did predate the war."

"And are you enjoying your new Stella?" He looked directly at her.

She wasn't quite sure what to say, and so she told the truth, if a bit reluctantly and not quite completely.

"Yes, yes. Of course. Actually, a friend will be keeping it for a while before returning it to me."

"Oh, Mr. Dean?" She was unaware he had met Jeffrey.

"No, another friend. You may have met him the night you were here."

He made no attempt to hide his interest.

"Henry Thurmond. Henry is a curator at the County Museum and a good friend. He's also a passionate Stella admirer and asked to borrow the print for a while."

"I hope he enjoys it," Diedrich said, looking again at the Grosz and then walking slowly about the gallery, examining the others. "Well, I must be going. I'll be calling you or seeing you in six weeks or so."

"I'll send the purchase papers to your address in New York, probably next week," Rachel told him. "And congratulations again. I'm certain it will give you quite a lot of pleasure."

A police car was in the driveway of their house when she arrived. One cop was in the car talking on the radio. The other—the same man who had responded to the call from the gallery earlier—was standing in the living room, writing his report. Jeffrey stood beside him.

"Nothing's gone that I can find," he said, "but I think you'd better have a look too."

"No appliances missing. No TV sets, VCRs or anything else that can be easily fenced?" The cop was a young man who was clearly beginning to have his doubts about Jeffrey and Rachel.

"I told you already. Nothing like that is missing." Jeffrey was having his own doubts too.

Minutes later, Rachel confirmed Jeffrey's opinion and once again the police left.

"Why move the furniture?" she asked. "I don't understand."

"The odd thing is the only furniture that's been

moved is furniture that was against the walls. And the beds have been pulled out. Somebody is looking for something."

"But what?"

"You tell me. It can't be small, because anyplace something small could be hidden hasn't been touched. Whatever it is, it fits behind a sofa or under a bed."

"A painting?"

"Yes. But why?" Jeffrey walked across the living room and adjusted his two prize Dickens novels, which had fallen and hit the end table when the sofa had been pulled out.

It was later that evening before she remembered she still hadn't reached Henry. A fire was burning in the fireplace and Jeffrey was sitting in his favorite chair engrossed in a book, his shoes off and his feet on the footstool. She too had been reading, but was less engrossed. She was catching up on her art journals and fighting off the uncomfortable feelings the events of the day were causing. She left the room and went to the phone.

"Henry's not at home. I left a message on his machine."

"What is it he said?" Jeffrey looked up and rubbed his eyes.

"He left a message while the people from the museum were in the gallery. He wanted to tell me something about the Stella. And about another one."

□□□ 13 ■

THAT NEXT afternoon, the day after the gallery and their house had been broken into, Henry's secretary called Rachel. Henry had not come to work that day or the previous one, and was not answering his home phone. She said for Henry not to call the office was highly unusual, and she added she knew Rachel and Henry were friends—Rachel thought something more than friendship was being implied, but she said nothing—and she wondered if Rachel had heard from him.

"No, no I haven't. But we've been trying to reach each other the last couple days."

"Oh." Not helpful, Rachel thought, but at least honest. "Well, if you hear from him would you tell him I canceled all his appointments for the day, but that the museum director is trying to get in touch with him?"

"I'll tell him." Rachel immediately called Henry's home number and left still another message with the answering machine.

"I'm getting very worried," she told Jeffrey that

night. They were in bed, about to go to sleep. She had just gotten home from a university speaking engagement, and he had been out to dinner and spent the evening with Mike, who was struggling mightily with a term paper on electronics—a subject that puzzled Jeffrey as much as it fascinated his son.

"I'm beginning to agree." He reached across to her and pulled her gently to his side.

"This isn't like him. You know it."

"I thought you might be worrying more because of what happened at the gallery and here," he said, and he could feel her shudder slightly.

"Maybe."

"Call again in the morning—early—and if you don't get him I'll go up to his house before I go to the office."

"I'll go with you."

The next morning there was still no Henry, so they dressed quickly and drove the fifteen minutes to his house, a trip requiring a brief burst of speed onto the Hollywood Freeway followed by the sharp narrow curves of the streets in the Hollywood Hills.

"He's there," Jeffrey said as soon as he saw the house. "That's his car in the driveway."

They rang the bell, and when there was no response they pounded on the door. Rachel peered into the mailbox and pulled out two days' worth of mail.

"Try the door," she said. "The alarm-system light is green—it's off."

Jeffrey hesitated, then turned the knob. As the door opened, Jeffrey's demeanor went from curious to wary, and a sense of foreboding filled them both.

They called Henry's name.

There was no response. Jeffrey stepped into the small entry hall and turned to the large living room overlooking the city. The first thing he saw in the bright winter sunlight was the skyline of Los Angeles. The next thing he saw was Henry's naked body lying face down on the carpet.

"Jesus Christ." Jeffrey turned and pushed Rachel back out of the front door.

He stepped back into the house to call the police. Rachel followed him, and when she saw Henry she gasped, grabbed Jeffrey, and, convulsed by grief and terror, began gasping for air. Seconds later she was swallowing hard, trying to hold down the vomit. The room smelled of death. She could hear Jeffrey calling the police. Then he quickly knelt beside the body, and took Henry's wrist in his hand to feel for a pulse. There was none.

They were standing by the front door, waiting, when they heard the sirens coming up the hill. Rachel was toward a corner of the porch, her cheeks streaked with tears. Jeffrey held her. It was a small area, no more than four by four, and they were immobilized by their fear and their grief. The first policeman in the door had to physically push them aside to get in.

"You found him?" the next cop asked.

"Yes," Jeffrey said, and Rachel nodded.

"You friends of his?"

"Good friends," Rachel said. They were led out to the street and to a plainclothes detective, who began asking them questions. He asked them rapidly, beginning with Henry's name, and he wrote down each of their responses. They watched as all the appropriate accoutrements of death arrived at the house: no comfort for the deceased, but a way for others to avoid seeing. A police pathologist arrived, followed by more detectives, and finally, the man from the coroner's office. It was also state-of-the-art police work: The equipment was shiny and new, the lab technician who traditionally used a still camera now came equipped with a video camera as well.

Another detective came out of the house and walked up to them. "Do you know the deceased's house well?" he asked. Jeffrey thought it oddly formal, stated that way, and horribly final. The deceased. The deceased was their friend.

"We knew Henry's house well."

"The body is covered now. If you don't mind, could you come into the house and look it over? Deaths like this tend to be robberies as well, and we want you to tell us if anything in particular is missing."

The house was perfectly in order, everything in its place, neat and clean as Henry kept it. So far as they could tell, nothing was missing. Jeffrey opened the stereo cabinet, and all of Henry's equipment was there, and when he saw it it began to occur to Jeffrey that something quite far from robbery had been going on in this otherwise orderly man's orderly life.

"Nothing?" the detective asked, puzzled. He seemed to doubt their assessment.

"Nothing," they both said at once. Rachel explained: "A lot of these things are valuable. He was a curator at the museum and something of a collector."

"The kind of people who do this sort of thing—with rare exceptions—don't know fine art. They know labels like Sony, RCA."

"I am quite sure everything is here," Rachel insisted.

Nothing appeared disturbed in the bedroom, either. Henry's suit was thrown across the bed, his socks, shoes, and underwear on the floor. His necktie was the first thing Jeffrey had seen: It was the only piece of clothing on his body, and it had been wrapped tightly around his neck.

The detectives questioned them for several more minutes, repeating many of the same questions.

"Do you know if he was homosexual?"

"I think so, yes." Rachel said.

Finally the detective ventured an opinion:

"Robbery is usually the most apparent motive, but not here. The other likely thing, which happens all too frequently in this part of town, is that it was a sex-related crime. But even then, robbery is usually part of it. Not this time, though—even his money is on his dresser."

"He was a good person," Jeffrey said. "Decent, honest."

"They usually are," the detective told him. "And lonely too."

Henry's covered body was carried out of the house an hour later and Rachel went in with a detective to look for Henry's telephone book to find his mother. Rachel remembered she lived in Indiana. While she looked, Jeffrey walked through the house, checking once again to see if anything was missing, and feeling all the time he was invading his friend's privacy, a feeling that prevailed despite the fact of death. Suddenly a thought struck him. He walked quickly through the house again. What he was looking for now wouldn't be easy to hide.

"The Stella," he said. "It's not here."

"The what?"

Rachel gasped. "No one would kill him for something like that!"

"Somebody killed him, and the Stella isn't here. I've been looking." Jeffrey paused, took Rachel's hand, and looked directly at the detective as he spoke to him. "It was an artwork, a print by Frank Stella. Rachel bought it, and she and Henry were sharing it. Henry took it with him when he left our house a couple of nights ago."

"And it isn't here," the detective concluded. As soon as he understood it was a work of art, and that it had value, he was interested. Definitely interested.

□□□ 14. ■

EDWARD ALVAREZ III was not an ordinary cop. He was very proud of that. In his ten years with the Los Angeles Police Department, he had put in the required time on a beat, in a patrol car, as duty officer, the works. But while other cops were off duty and drinking in the dives they cherished, Edward Alvarez III was in school. Other cops had beer, women, and each other for their recreation; he had books. He loved knowledge and was not in the least afraid to use it. At first he had hid his passion, but not for long.

He was shorter than most of his fellows and rounder, but there was no fat on him. He was compact, in excellent condition, his body as primed as his mind. He had grown up on the streets of the East Los Angeles barrio, under the watchful eye of his mother and the stern, protective discipline of his father. He and his six sisters had all done well for themselves. That was their way out of poverty and second-class citizenship, and it had been drilled into them since they were barely out of diapers.

If there was a cloud on his horizon, it was one of conflict. As the only son in a devoutly Catholic family, he
was, at thirty-two, unmarried. By choice. He didn't want
a wife and children cluttering his life, at least not yet. The
time would come, but until then his mother was given to
issuing great dramatic sighs when the subject came up—
and it often did, because she brought it up. His father
handled the contretemps with baleful looks, and, typically, without words. His sisters, four of whom were
married, had cheerfully chided him and promised to provide the grandchildren he had yet to produce. So far there
were seven of them.

His family had even become accustomed to his
strange interests. His father had urged him to be a dentist—be his own boss—and his mother, after a lifetime of
too little money, had encouraged accounting. Both
thought the LAPD was a great way to finance higher education. But not an art education. Eddie Alvarez—they
called him Eduardo at home—had discovered the visual
image as a youngster and had never stopped pursuing his
fascination with it. In nine years he would be eligible for
retirement from the police department, and long before
that he was going to have his credential to teach art history at the college level. And teach he would.

He had gone to night school at Cal State Northridge,
six years of it, to get his bachelor's degree. His master's
took much less time but cost a great deal more. He had
enrolled in USC's master-of-fine-arts program. It had
been expensive but worth every cent. His work there
earned him a minority scholarship in the university's
prestigious Ph.D. program.

He was now about two years of part-time classes and
a completed thesis short of his doctorate. The education
had already paid off, at least as far as Eddie was concerned, with a singular position as a cop. He was at-

tached, most of the time, to the bunco-forgery division, and his specialty was questioned documents. He himself was not an expert, and he was the first to admit it. But he knew where to find one. He had the name of every expert on forgery in Southern California, knew most of them on a first-name basis, and he knew others throughout the country. Eddie Alvarez was more at home ferreting through the archives at the Getty museum than he was at his standard-issue desk at police headquarters.

When he had first been assigned to the newly created job five years before, it had been as a part-timer. Even in a city as big and rich as Los Angeles there had not been all that much to occupy him. When he wasn't at his preferred work, he was a burglary detective. He pursued the one as energetically as he did the other, for he knew that unless he did well as a detective he could not continue with his chosen work.

He also knew it was just a matter of time until it would become a full-time job. In the last five years the museum and art activity in Los Angeles had exploded. The L.A. County Museum of Art had added an architectural curiosity to its hodgepodge of buildings, nearly doubling its exhibition space. The new Museum of Contemporary Art had blossomed in a converted police garage in Little Tokyo into an instant success, and was now operating both its old garage, known as the Temporary Contemporary, and a magnificent new building at the top of Bunker Hill. If that wasn't enough, the Getty museum had passed from the watchful, stringent supervision of J. Paul Getty to the terms of his will, and was now the richest museum in the country, perhaps the world. It had extraordinary research facilities, a crowded little museum overlooking the ocean at Malibu, and, within the next several years, would construct a permanent facility in the Santa Monica Mountains, looking down from its own Mount Olympus onto the rest of the city.

Los Angeles was a city of trends. Eddie knew that from growing up unnoticed but observant in the city itself. When the little knots of children were duly trotted through museums by their schoolteachers, Eddie was always watching. And he watched still. People, particularly people with money and social ambitions, followed trends like so many bejeweled lemmings, eventually plummeting from the weight of their own ambition. As the museum world expanded, so did the more scattered world of collectors. They were among the most gullible people he had ever met. In their rush to have the finest—from the Old World and the New—they were in an even bigger rush to find a bargain. They sometimes got what they paid for, and that's where Eddie Alvarez came in.

He had learned of Henry's murder some time after it had happened, and only after Jeffrey had discovered the Frank Stella print was missing. As soon as he was informed of this, Eddie had a full-color reproduction of the print in a book on his desk, and considerable information about it, including the number of prints made as well as the address and telephone numbers for both the artist and the printer who had made the original. He had filled out the appropriate form, asking for information on any similar murders or thefts in other cities, and had taken it himself down to the department's computer.

He had known Henry Thurmond only slightly. He had twice heard him speak at the museum and had once taken him to lunch, the purpose of which had been to determine Henry's expertise and his potential usefulness to his work. He remembered him as an intelligent, polite, even gracious man with a wry sense of humor and someone who was not at all surprised to find a short, swarthy Mexican-American with considerable education and knowledge. Eddie always remembered those who treated him as a social and intellectual equal. There hadn't been all that many.

He flipped through his telephone book, a bound volume where each entry had its own page. He looked under "books and autographs" and found Jeffrey Dean's name, address, and telephone number, along with a short paragraph of neatly written notes about Dean's areas of knowledge.

They had met only once, at a rare-book convention a few years back when Alvarez had materialized after Dean turned up two forged Steinbeck first editions, and the detective had demanded they be taken off the market. Dean had been right, they had been forgeries, but Alvarez did not remember the details of what subsequently happened.

Eddie Alvarez met Jeffrey Dean for the second time the day after Henry's body was discovered. It was the first time he had ever met Rachel Sabin. Their rendezvous took place in the atrium at the big new County Museum building, next to a waterfall the architects had designed to make climbing a lot of stairs less strenuous. Alvarez did not like the new building. Jeffrey and Rachel expressed mild disapproval, and with that and Henry's death in common, they had shaken hands.

Eddie, who missed very little, studied his companions. Jeffrey was composed, in control and watchful. She was nervous, glancing about the large lobby and uncertain how to act, yet obviously intelligent. Eddie thought perhaps Jeffrey's years as a journalist made it a bit easier to deal with what was happening, while her experience as an academic and an art dealer made it somewhat less tolerable.

"He was your friend?"

"Yes," Rachel answered. "And we hoped one day to be in business together."

"How long had you known him?" Alvarez had read the reports from the detectives who interviewed Jeffrey and Rachel, and he knew all of their answers already. Yet, like most thorough police officers, he wanted to hear them for himself.

"A little less than a year. We met when he gave me some advice about a collection of art I had, and that was the beginning."

"That collection would be the George Grosz show at your gallery?"

"Yes." Rachel seemed surprised he knew so much. "I—we—" she said, glancing at Jeffrey, "decided to donate one painting to the museum. That's when we met Henry."

"How did he come to have the Stella print?"

Rachel explained, with Jeffrey sketching in details, about the opening of the show, the meeting with Karl Diedrich, the purchase of the print from him, and of Henry's picking the print to keep for a year.

"Have you seen Diedrich since he sold you the Stella?"

"Once. He came to look at the Grosz drawing he had bought."

"Did he mention the Stella at that time?"

"Yes, as a matter of fact he did." She paused, trying to recollect their conversation. "He asked where it was, and I told him about Henry."

"Anything else?"

"Yes. He mentioned Jeffrey. I assumed they had met at the opening of the show."

Eddie's look at Jeffrey was a question.

"I don't recall meeting him," Jeffrey answered, "but then I met quite a few people that night."

Finding the print had been easy. As soon as Jeffrey had realized it was missing, Rachel had wondered if

Henry was having it reframed. Eddie then did the obvious. He telephoned the museum, and located the print in the museum framer's workshop. Henry's secretary, a middle-aged woman clearly distraught and still in shock over Henry's murder, appeared and escorted the three of them to Henry's office. There, out of its frame and in a storage folder, was the Stella. Also there was an elderly man wearing a tie and a lab coat. His name was Arnoldo Tellini. He had a dense, almost whimsical Italian accent and had gained his arcane knowledge of restoration in the course of a long apprenticeship at a number of Italian museums.

"The Stella," he said, tilting his head in the direction of the print, ". . . it is a forgery."

Eddie watched Jeffrey and Rachel, let their reactions register. Both were clearly astounded, and he instinctively knew their emotions were genuine. He had already known about the forgery, and had spoken at length with Tellini that morning.

"How did you discover it?" Jeffrey asked.

"Very simple, really, if you have the resources. I have a new set of chemicals for testing prints, and the museum has a carbon-dating facility. The carbon dating isn't very important for a print that is less than fifteen years old. It will, however, tell the order in which the ink was applied in the printing. The printer, as instructed by Stella, who"—Tellini's English faltered for a moment—"attended the printing itself, was to apply the coral after the pink. In this it was applied first."

Tellini made a theatrical gesture at the folder, and began unwrapping it. "Also, my new chemicals, which are experimental only, help determine more exactly the composition of the ink. When the print was made in 1971, this color ink"—he pointed to one nearly triangular section of pale turquoise in the series of protractor forms on the print—"was difficult if not almost impossible to print in this clarity and shade. It required a special mixture, a compound, and even then you can find some variation in the other prints."

He looked with considerable satisfaction at the print itself. He did not seem offended that it was a fake, merely satisfied that he had found it out.

"And?" Rachel was somewhat more familiar with Tellini's information than either Jeffrey or Eddie.

"The ink used on this print is actually an acrylic paint. It provides a perfect, even color and savings of many hours of work."

"But why?" Jeffrey asked.

Tellini answered with a shrug of his shoulders, and raised hands, his fingers spread in indecision. "Who knows? Money probably."

"I mean why did you test it? Did Henry suspect it was fake?"

"No, no, not at all. The discovery is . . . strictly . . . an accident. I had my new chemicals, maybe two weeks, and I was waiting for a print to be reframed so that I could test them. The framer stopped me in the hall, told me about the Stella, and I went to get my chemicals.

"That's what Henry's idea for the Stella was—to reframe it. But surely a fake, or two prints with the same number, would eventually show up," Jeffrey argued.

"Eventually can be a long time," Eddie said evenly. "And there are lots of people with the money to buy what they want, keep it where they want, and not really care if it's a fake. Most don't ever know. There are plenty of people eager to own contemporary art."

"So instead of seventy of these prints, there are now seventy-one."

"Oh no, I'm certain there are more than this," Eddie corrected him. "It takes too much time to forge just one

print. I've never known of just one. More always turn
up. And Stella is a very popular artist."

"Henry died for this?" Rachel was angry.

"That's what doesn't make sense," Eddie said evenly.
"He already had it, you had already paid for it. Why get
it back? We've had Mr. Tellini here go over it thoroughly, and there's nothing else to it that we know of."

"Well, then?" Rachel wasn't willing to accept such a
simple answer. There was more and she knew it. So did
Jeffrey.

"Every work of art, real or fake, has a past."

"What's the past . . . of this?" Jeffrey stared at the
print.

"We can make an informed guess. Mr. Tellini says the
ink used on this is manufactured in Germany, and that
very likely is where the print was made. The Germans
have probably the finest presses in the world."

"Maybe Henry was killed for some other reason and
the print had nothing to do with it." Rachel hoped it was
so, but she knew better.

"Possibly, but a very remote possibility, Miss Sabin,"
Eddie explained. "Your gallery was broken into and
nothing was taken, and so was your home. Somebody
was looking for something, and this no doubt was it."

"Karl Diedrich?"

Eddie nodded. Jeffrey stood still. Rachel had the uncomprehending look of someone who has just had the
wind knocked out of her. Suspicion was one thing, confirmation quite another.

☐☐☐ 15. ■

RACHEL'S PROFESSION equipped her with excellent
powers of observation and description, and she was able
to provide a very accurate description of Karl Diedrich.
Eddie, who shared her ability, took detailed notes.

"What do you do next?" Jeffrey asked him.

"I'm going to follow procedures . . . at first. Then
I'm going to bend the rules a bit. Will the two of you be
available later this afternoon if I need you?"

Eddie did not elaborate on his plan, and his statement
seemed more final than an invitation to further questions,
and so Jeffrey and Rachel drove back over the hill to go
about their business for the day. It wasn't easy. They
both had questions for which there were no answers, and
they shared a common bond of anger and sorrow over
Henry's death. The death of a close friend under such circumstances always leaves survivors with a sliding scale of
reactions that, for most, finally settle on acceptance.
Rachel mourned, Jeffrey wanted revenge. Each shared the
other's emotion, and neither knew how to react.

Eddie Alvarez's profession gave him some immunity to emotion, and it also gave him a determination to go about his work with renewed vigor. While Jeffrey and Rachel drove north through the torturous curves of Laurel Canyon back to the San Fernando Valley, Eddie headed west on Wilshire Boulevard, threading his way through the canyon of high-rises and traffic to the Federal Building at Wilshire and Sepulveda. He took his file from his car seat, patted it reassuringly, and rode the elevator to the FBI headquarters. This was an official visit.

The FBI offices were not unlike Eddie's at LAPD: standard government issue with cream-colored walls, all purposefully impersonal. A picture of the President hung on the wall near the information desk. Within minutes Eddie was sitting comfortably beside the desk of Greg Nathanson, an FBI agent he had worked with on several occasions before, and whom he admired. The feeling was mutual. Nathanson was a California native, and, unlike most in his service, he had not been moved every two years to a new post. Nathanson knew the West, and knew how to work it. Eddie opened his file and explained his problem.

"Nothing besides a name and a description?" Nathanson asked when Eddie was finished.

"That's it."

"OK, let's go." Nathanson pushed back his chair and started down the long institutional hall. Eddie followed. Finally, they stepped into a room full of computer terminals, where a young Japanese-American woman listened carefully to them both before turning to her terminal.

Diedrich's name and description was sent to the FBI's main computer terminal in Washington, where it was processed in detail, each bit of information matched to similar descriptions stored in the computer's massive memory. The procedure took less than twenty minutes, and, as Eddie expected, nothing was found.

"Nada," Nathanson muttered as he strode back to his desk. "But I'll keep looking."

"I'll be in touch," Eddie responded. He rode the elevator back to the lobby, then walked across to the bank of elevators that serviced the higher floors of the building. This was an unofficial visit.

The offices of the Central Intelligence Agency were as institutional as the FBI's and could have been interchangeable with them. Only the occupants were different. The FBI dealt with situations within the United States and its territories. The CIA was prohibited by law from operating in the United States, just as the FBI was prohibited from invading the CIA's turf, which was the rest of the world.

Bureaucracy survives on procedure and order, and many encumbered by it also know how to circumvent it. Eddie knew that the rules required him to relay his request first to the FBI and then, if nothing was found, to ask the FBI to consult the CIA. It was a sensible rule, but one that did not take into consideration personalities and the fact that the CIA and FBI had a long and traditional animosity preventing them from cooperating easily, all the more so over a small request from a local cop. Eddie knew better. He also knew a CIA agent.

Mark Joseph was as tall and lean as Eddie was short and thick, as blond and fair as Eddie was dark. There the dissimilarities ended. Mark and Eddie shared a passion for their work, a devotion to knowledge, and a fanatic loyalty to the Dodgers. They went to games together at least a dozen times each year.

Joseph greeted his friend expansively. Eddie, normally gregarious and friendly, withheld enough of his enthusiasm so that Joseph picked up on it immediately. "I sense this is a business visit."

"Right."

"And off the record because it's against the rules."

"Right."

"Shoot."

Once again, Eddie told his story.

"What can I do?"

"I don't think the man's name is Karl Diedrich, but we all believe he is German. I would like to see a picture of every German who has diplomatic status in this country."

"All right, what else?"

"Just that. Somewhere to start."

"You think this is something more than just a local con artist working his trade?"

"Yes. I don't know why for sure. The forgery expert says the printing was probably done in Germany. This guy is German."

"Then I think I should get you the diplomatic lists from the Federal Republic and the DDR, in case he shows up there."

Another trip down a long hall and another consultation with a woman sitting before a computer followed.

"The information you're after is actually the property of the State Department, but we can access their computer," Joseph explained.

"Mark, I'm beginning to think there are no secrets in this world."

"You'd be surprised," Joseph said, smiling.

They were told it would take at least an hour before access to the State Department computer was complete, and almost another hour before the photographs could be set on the Rapifax system from Washington.

"Lunch?" Eddie suggested.

"Yes, but first I want to make one call. I know someone downstairs in the Secret Service passport control division. I'll have them feed the name into their computer and see if anyone named Karl Diedrich has left the country in the last several days.

"Everybody has a computer," Eddie said.

"So do you cops," Joseph countered.

"So do most smart criminals."

Two hours, two beers, and a meal later—Mark called it a "civil service forty-five minute lunch break"—Eddie and Mark were back in the Federal Building, staring at a stack of some five hundred photographs on Mark's desk. They were mounted four to each eight-by-ten Rapifax sheet.

"That ought to keep you busy for a while," Mark teased.

"Not me. I've never seen the guy. But I have two people who have."

"This is like dynamiting a fish pond," Jeffrey said, when Eddie showed them the pile of photographs.

"I don't understand," Eddie smiled.

"Throw a stick of dynamite into a fish pond, and a few seconds later stunned fish will float to the surface. We're looking for one stunned fish in particular."

"I see. I'll throw the dynamite, the two of you can do the looking."

The pile of pictures was on the low table in front of their sofa. All three leaned forward, ready to begin their inspection. It was early evening. The Santa Anas had blown themselves out, and a damp cold had settled in. Winter had returned to Southern California, yet its chill was nowhere near as bone deep as the chill Rachel felt an hour later when she came upon the photograph of Karl Diedrich about three fourths of the way through the big pile.

"That's him."

Jeffrey confirmed it. "I remember him now. He didn't stay long."

"But he came back the next day. And once again after that. I'm certain this is him," Rachel said, looking at Eddie to see what he was going to do next.

There was a small block of type underneath each picture. The one under the photograph of the man who called himself Karl Diedrich said his name was Wolfgang Dieter, attached to the cultural-affairs office of the Deutsche Demokratische Republik mission to the United Nations. The rest of the information gave the statistics printed on his passport, including his passport number.

Eddie Alvarez wasted no time. He telephoned Mark Joseph at his home, read him the name and passport number, then quickly hung up the phone. Ten minutes later the phone rang and Eddie, without asking permission, answered it.

"When? Shit. OK, Mark, thanks. If he comes back you'll let us know? Fine. I see."

"We missed him," Eddie said, looking at his watch, "and just by hours. He left the country on a flight to Warsaw about six hours ago. Gone."

"What now?" Jeffrey asked.

"Where will you two be tomorrow if I need you?"

"Same places," Rachel said. "And afterward we'll be here."

"You've heard of the International Foundation for Art Research, Rachel?" Eddie, accustomed to conducting all his police business more formally, with last names, had agreed—at Rachel and Jeffrey's insistence—to address them by their first names. At first he had felt uncomfortable, and had several times reverted to "Mr. Dean" and "Miss Sabin," only to be corrected with a smile. He now found he was comfortable with them. He was even beginning to like them.

"Yes, of course. I subscribe to their bulletins."

"I'm the Los Angeles representative. It's an informal arrangement, which means I am not paid for it. I've been active in the organization since I started this work. I think they asked me because I'm the only cop here who is actually qualified."

"Good enough reason," Jeffrey said. "Can I get you some wine or some beer? We're going to have a drink before dinner."

Eddie wavered.

"Is there some sort of rule against it?" Rachel asked.

"As a matter of fact, yes."

"Good. Then that makes two rules you broke today," Jeffrey said.

"Two?"

"You weren't supposed to go to the CIA yourself, right?"

"Right."

"That's the other. Now which will it be—wine or beer?"

"Beer."

"Dos Equis all right with you?"

"Well, well. You bet."

□□□ 16 ■

A TALL, fair man with wire-rimmed glasses and an almost austere presence stood behind Eddie Alvarez the next morning when Jeffrey opened his office door. Eddie introduced him as Mark Joseph of the CIA.

"Oh, no," Jeffrey said. Joseph smiled at him.

"Is Miss Sabin in today?" Joseph asked evenly.

"I'll buzz her and she'll be right up. Would you like coffee or tea?" She appeared in seconds, confident and appraising.

"Coffee, please," Joseph said. Eddie nodded and smiled—he hoped it was a reassuring smile that included Rachel and Jeffrey and not Joseph.

Jeffrey expected Joseph would do the talking first, and so did Rachel. Both were mildly surprised when Joseph quickly deferred to Eddie. And both noticed beads of sweat on Eddie's usually composed forehead.

"I've done some checking," he began. "Quite a bit of it. And I have several things to tell you. If you recall our conversation at the museum, I said then that I felt—given the complications of producing a forgery such as Mr. Thurmond's Stella—it was very likely there were others." Eddie paused.

"It wasn't Henry's Stella," Rachel corrected him. "It was mine. I bought it, Henry borrowed it."

"That's right," Eddie admitted.

"And we both feel responsible for what happened," Jeffrey added. He noticed a quick look of approval pass from Joseph to Eddie.

They both nodded. Rachel, who had been sitting on the edge of one of the wing-back chairs that faced Jeffrey's desk, slid back into it as if to hide her remorse.

"I have found some of the others. An art gallery in Chicago has turned up three of them. It seems the print numbers were wrong on one of the fake prints, so the owner began checking."

"Stellas, like ours?" Rachel interrupted.

"No, newer. From the *Had Gadya* series."

"Jesus." Jeffrey was beginning to feel no work of art was sacred. "We have one of those too."

Rachel was suddenly afraid to speak or to move. She knew she should be offering more coffee, but she could not. Instead she glanced at Jeffrey.

"Do you think our Stella from the *Had Gadya* is a fake?"

"I think you ought to have it examined," Eddie said evenly. "Where did you buy it?"

"From a dealer down in Venice. A very reliable man, who is also a friend."

"Where did he get it?"

"From the printer."

"You've probably got the real thing, but I still suggest you have it checked."

"How did you find this out?"

"Through the International Foundation for Art Research—I mentioned that to you before as well. They keep a listing of all fakes and thefts, and the Chicago Stellas were there. That's all they have right now, but I assure you, there are others."

"Miss Sabin," Joseph interrupted, speaking for the first time. "Could you give Detective Alvarez the name and address of the gallery where you bought your Stella?"

"Which one?"

"Dieter sold you the smaller one, correct?"

"Yes."

"Where did he say he got it?"

"From a client in Santa Barbara."

"That print," Eddie interrupted, "was purchased from a San Francisco dealer nearly a week ago." He looked down and consulted his notes. "Printed in 1971, number sixty-eight of seventy."

"Which was it, a fake or the original?" Jeffrey asked.

"No way to know for certain," Eddie told him. "But in all likelihood it was the original. The gallery had purchased it from a collector, a collector who had bought it new in 1971, direct from a Stella dealer."

Jeffrey and Rachel didn't make any attempt to hide their distress.

"And the larger Stella?" Joseph asked.

She knew the gallery from memory, and gave him the owner's name and telephone number as well.

Eddie paused. "I know them to be reliable."

"They are," Rachel said. "I don't think there will be any problem with the big Stella." Still, she wondered if she would ever walk past the big print in her living room without thinking of Henry. Stella, by association.

Once again, Eddie consulted his notes. "The coroner's report on Henry Thurmond states he had been dead something over twenty-four hours—longer than we had supposed. Clearly Dieter had already made the exchange because the print at the museum—which Mr. Thurmond wanted reframed—was a fake."

"Did Henry know it?"

"Probably not. But he could recognize Dieter and that was enough to get him killed."

They all fell silent, lost in their own troubled speculations.

"I am here"—Joseph paused, choosing his words carefully—"because we know now that whatever is happening, it does not involve local forgery or even forgery in this country—so far as we've been able to determine. It does involve a citizen of the DDR, an East German who was traveling in this country on a diplomatic passport. That's where we come in."

"Where do we come in?" Jeffrey asked pointedly.

"You are the only people known to have had dealings with Wolfgang Dieter—Karl Diedrich. That is, outside of his known contacts as part of his United Nations work. I am certain there are others, but so far we've been unable to find them."

"And?"

"And, as such, you are our most direct link to him."

"What does that mean?" Rachel asked. Joseph paused, as if to collect his thoughts. "Exactly mean," she added.

"There is more, and then I'll answer your question, Miss Sabin. I'll answer it as exactly as I possibly can." He was sitting on a hard bentwood chair, a formal man who did not seem comfortable in the informal life of California. He placed his hands on his knees, stretched his long arms, and continued.

"When Detective Alvarez came to me with his request, I honored it. Immediately. This is not the custom when our two"—he turned toward Eddie—"when our two areas mix. I did it because I had reason to do it, reason to ignore the more formal aspects of the rules and regulations which govern requests made from one area of law enforcement to another. My reason was simply because a foreign national was involved. It's that simple."

"And you discovered it was Dieter." Rachel found a logical comfort in stating the obvious.

"We also know Dieter is connected with the United Nations, with the DDR's cultural program, but we also suspect—suspect strongly—that he is a member of their secret service. In fact, the suspicion, now that we've checked with our Berlin people, is that he's also connected with the KGB."

"What would someone like him be doing selling art forgeries?" Jeffrey wondered.

"Exactly," Joseph said. "What does it mean? I had a long conversation late last night with our head of station in Berlin. Dieter is in his files as well, because he crosses regularly from the eastern sector into the West. Only highly placed—and very trusted—East Germans are allowed free access to the West."

"He must have gone directly from Warsaw to East Berlin."

"Correct. We would like to discover what he's doing dealing in art forgeries. It could be that this is Mr. Dieter's extra-curricular activity, his way of making money. But it's unlikely. Our feeling is that there is a connection between the art forgeries and his . . . his government work. We'd like to find out."

"How do you propose doing that?" Jeffrey asked. He noticed Eddie was suddenly uncomfortable, fidgeting in his chair. He was staring at the rows of books neatly lined up on bookshelves, as if searching for a particular title instead of concentrating on the conversation taking place.

"There are two ways. We can begin a painstaking and

long investigation into whatever is going on. That could take weeks or even months, and may not turn up anything." He paused. Jeffrey and Rachel both knew it was a deliberate pause, and Jeffrey in some distant recess of his mind sensed what was coming next.

"Or we could warm things up for him, warm them up quite a bit. One reason for doing that is it appears Dieter doesn't leave many witnesses behind when he's working in this country. My suspicion is that your friend Henry Thurmond was not his first victim, nor will he be the last."

"What he's saying . . . and why he's here is that he believes both of you to be in some danger," Eddie interrupted, his attention suddenly diverted from the shelves of books. "You know about the forgery and you know about Dieter, or at least you've had some dealings with him."

"You also have expertise in art," Joseph added for emphasis. Then he took off on another tack. "Mr. Thurmond was an innocent in this. Far more innocent than either of you . . . especially you, Miss Sabin. I do not mean to imply that you are in any sort of collusion with Dieter—I mean only that you've had business dealings with him."

The marginal thought in Jeffrey's mind had begun to form solid proportions. "How do you propose 'warming things up a bit for him . . . warming them up quite a bit'?"

"I have told you Dieter crosses into West Berlin frequently. Sometimes as many as four times a week. We also know he frequents a number of art galleries there. We want to talk to him. Very much, in fact. We propose the two of you go to Berlin, pretend to be on business, and that you go shopping at those same galleries. And, of course, we're going to also suggest you ask after Mr. Dieter."

Neither Jeffrey nor Rachel spoke. After a moment, Joseph continued.

"The danger is minimal. My colleagues have a much freer reign in Berlin than they do in other foreign cities, because Berlin is still an occupied city. You will be followed closely at all times. If it works as we propose, Dieter will be discovered. He'll either reveal what he's up to in his panic, or he'll close down the whole thing. We'd like to know exactly what he's up to, but failing that we'd also like to frighten him into shutting it all down. What do you think?"

"Why can't the CIA do it?" Rachel thought she knew the answer, but she wasn't certain.

"Easy. We need a real art expert. And they know that's what you are."

"I think we'd like to have some time to think it over," Jeffrey said evenly. He felt two strong emotions, the first a desire to pursue Dieter exactly as Joseph suggested, the other to protect himself and Rachel from danger by staying right where they were. Rachel felt much the same, though she also had a desire to find the answers for her friend Henry.

"You say we will be protected if we go to Berlin."

Joseph nodded.

"And that we are in some danger here, at home. Will we be protected here?"

"The CIA is prevented by law from operating inside the country. I'm sure you know that."

"What about the FBI?" Jeffrey's question was emphatic.

"We can always ask," Joseph remarked diplomatically. "I'm certain they will be interested." He paused. "Minimally."

"Things just sort of fall between the cracks when one of you hands off to the other, is that what you're saying?"

"In a sense, yes. Though not as bad as you make it sound."

Eddie took out a handkerchief and carefully wiped his brow. His discomfort was palpable.

"We'll think about it." Rachel spoke as she stood, indicating the meeting was finished.

□□□ 17 ■

THAT NIGHT, Rachel cooked omelets while Jeffrey mixed a big salad. They were uncharacteristically silent while they worked in their kitchen. It was a time when they normally shared the events of the day with one another, but what was shared this night was unspoken. Neither had yet figured out how best to talk about it. It was raining steadily, a safe, enclosing winter rain that seemed to seal them off from the world outside their house.

"Let's eat in the living room. I'll build a fire."

"Better hurry, the omelets are almost done."

Jeffrey took their wineglasses and the place settings from the small kitchen table and placed them on the cocktail table. He put logs into the fireplace and lit the gas jet. As he turned to go back into the kitchen he looked up at the big Stella print on the wall. He was still staring at it when Rachel came in, carrying their dinner on a tray. She was wearing dark-brown wool slacks and the beige cashmere sweater he had bought for her in London, and from the outside she seemed composed and organized, a woman enjoying a night at home with the man in her life.

Midway through the meal she put her fork down and leaned back against the sofa. "I can't eat."

Jeffrey leaned back too, placing his arm around her and pulling her to him. He kissed her gently.

"You taste like omelet."

"Is that a proposition?"

"Yes."

"I accept."

They sat in silence, watching the fire. Finally, Jeffrey stood up and crossed to the gas jet beside the fireplace. The fire was burning well on its own, so he turned the jet off. Then he sat in the chair next to the fireplace, his favorite chair, the place he liked best for reading and thinking.

"The CIA man, what exactly was he saying?" Rachel asked.

"He wasn't exactly saying anything. That's how they are. What I believe he was saying is that they want our help. They'll provide protection, but only up to a point."

"What point?"

"We'll be safer in Berlin. They'll see to it."

"I don't much like those people."

They fell silent. Jeffrey stared at the fire, Rachel at the Stella. It wasn't a fake, she was sure of it. But she was going to call up the man at the museum and ask him to test it, just to make sure.

"What do you think Henry would have done?" he said finally.

She smiled slightly. "Henry would have thought the whole thing was crazy. I imagine he would have walked away from it all."

"Even if it was you?"

"What do you mean?"

"If it was you who had been killed?"

She was silent, and he answered for her.

"I think he would have gone to Berlin."

"What do you think we ought to do?"

"The same. God knows, I don't feel any particular debt to the CIA or to any of those people. But I do feel an obligation to Henry. If it means catching his murderer, then I'm for it. If we can help stop some sneaky, dirty intrigue at the same time, so much the better."

"I don't know. I like things the way they are . . . or were. I don't know if I want to do something which just might be dangerous."

They both watched the fire for several more moments. Rachel finally continued her conversation, almost as if she'd never interrupted it.

"Yet I understand the only way we can get everything back to the way it was, was before all this started, is to go to Berlin and get it over with. I can do some work there as well. Can you?"

"I suppose. Not much, but a little. I've got a couple of customers in Berlin."

"How odd. We're deciding whether or not to undertake this . . . this thing . . . on the basis of business we can do while we're there."

"Don't feel bad. It's a way of dealing with unusual things—to concentrate on the everyday things we know better." He stopped, watched her, then stood up and began clearing the dishes. "It's how people are, Rachel. We deal with what we don't understand by thinking of what we know. And we deal with death by affirming life."

"I know."

"I want to make love to you. Affirm us."

She smiled at him, brushing her long black hair away from her eyes. "First, the dishes. Then I have some work to do."

"Me too."

He retreated into the bedroom he had converted into a den and office, and paid household bills. As their life together had settled into a routine, the various chores had been evenly divided. She had acquired the financing of the household, he the responsibility for its maintenance inside and outside. Rachel had grown up in New York and shared little of his pleasure in gardening. There were a few, less traditional divisions: Rachel showed an ability—Jeffrey thought of it as a talent—for arranging car repairs. She did it without anger and without problems, and invariably with good results. It amused him to watch mechanics react when he pulled up in his BMW and she followed in her Volvo to issue instructions on what to do with his car. He, in turn, impressed her with energetic participation in cleaning the house. It was, he said, one of his fetishes.

When he put the final stamp on the final envelope and piled the bills on the dresser next to his wallet, he returned to the living room and sat down to read. She was already there, her work spread before her, her reading glasses—a recent concession she permitted only Jeffrey to observe—perched on the end of her nose.

An hour later, he stepped out of the shower, toweled himself off, and, after a brief glance at the pajamas folded neatly on his closet shelf, slipped naked into bed. He was drifting off to sleep when he heard the rustle of the comforter and felt her hand come to rest at the base of his stomach, felt the tingle as her fingers petted his hair. He turned to her, felt her nipples brush against his chest, and smelled the sweetness in her hair.

He kissed her, gently at first and with more intensity as she responded to him. He kissed her neck, her ears, her breasts. She touched him gently with her fingertips, brushing them against his lips, his eyes, his chest, and eventually his penis and testicles. She called them angel kisses. He felt exactly as though he were being kissed by an angel.

Finally, he was on his back, gasping, and she was astride him, pulling him to her, moaning with pleasure. He let out a joyful yell as he came, his legs shaking violently. She kept on until her sharp, small cries ended. Then she lay beside him.

He reached over and wiped the perspiration from her forehead, then kissed her gently.

"I love you," he whispered.

"Please, God. Don't let anything bad happen," she said finally before she went to sleep.

□□□ 18 ∎

"THERE. WHISKEY, Coca-Cola, and champagne. Only vodka is missing."

"What are you talking about?" Rachel was in the throes of jet lag, lying on their bed, a pillow over her face to hide the sunlight, feeling mentally and physically paralyzed from the long, long flight. She peered out in the direction of the small refrigerator, assuming Jeffrey was taking stock of its contents.

Jeffrey was energized, shot awake by the cold, wintry Berlin air, the light snow falling across the city. He wasn't at the refrigerator. He was standing at the window, looking out on the small barren park that faced the entrance of the Steigenberger hotel. He had a guidebook in his hand.

"Come here and see."

Rachel, feeling every inch a martyr to her body, struggled off the bed and went to the window.

"Look."

"I don't see any whiskey, Coca-Cola, or champagne."

"Yes you do. There are three flags flying in front of the hotel. Name the countries."

"England, America, France."

"Right. According to this, the NATO phonetic guide refers to them as 'whiskey,' 'Coca-Cola,' and 'champagne': three of the four sectors of Berlin. The other is 'vodka' . . . the Russians."

"I got out of bed for that?"

"Where else will you find something like this? Here we are, in the only occupied city left from World War Two. No German flag flies here; the Russians won't allow it. Even Lufthansa is prohibited from flying into Berlin."

"I saw a Lufthansa jet sitting on the runway at the airport."

"It's an old plane, a museum for children. It's there as a reminder that Berlin is part of Germany, regardless of who occupies the city."

"Did you get that out of the guidebook too?"

"No, from the Pan Am pilot I was talking to at the airport in Frankfurt. He was deadheading back into Berlin."

"I really don't think these people need lessons in national pride."

"Probably not."

Rachel went to unpack, only to discover that while she had been lying down Jeffrey had done it all. Her clothes were hung neatly in the closet along with his, her toiletries stacked on the counter in the bathroom, the rest of her clothing in the drawers of the dresser. She had the most accessible part of the small closet, the biggest counter space in the bathroom, and the top drawers in the dresser. She wondered, not for the first time, if Jeffrey had always been so considerate.

They had traveled from Los Angeles to New York,

where they retreated for several hours into the TWA Ambassador Club. Jeffrey maintained his membership, not so much from a love of comfort but from a lifelong anxiety about airport waiting rooms. The sight of one passenger lying down in any airport was enough to convince him he'd never arrive at his destination. After several hours' layover, they flew all night to Frankfurt. The flight across the Atlantic was not a long one—just under seven hours, but it went through six time zones, making the night pitifully short and the dawn, minutes before they landed, very disorienting. Jeffrey had slept for four hours, while Rachel had tried—and failed—to sleep.

In the Frankfurt airport, Rachel huddled miserably with their luggage while Jeffrey walked through the shops that occupied most of the main building of the terminal. He had reported, with some interest, on the food, the cameras, and the fact that there was also an adult shop, with wall-to-wall pornography and sexual aids.

The Pan Am shuttle flight into Berlin had roused Rachel out of her stupor. Because it was traveling through East German airspace, the old 727 was restricted to an altitude of ten thousand feet, possibly the last trip in the jet age where it was possible to get a good look at the passing land. They watched the snow-covered landscape move by, then noted with interest the border, with its barbed wire, guard towers, and the large cleared path alongside it. On its approach to Tegel Airport, the plane crossed over into East Berlin.

It was a striking contrast. West Berlin was jammed with new buildings and there was considerable traffic on the streets. In an instant, the topography changed to sparse traffic and buildings that appeared from the air to be either ruins or in disrepair. They both saw the wall at the moment they crossed it, and then remarked—as passengers have for years—on the one oddity in the East

Berlin landscape: the East German television tower poked high into the sky, its bulbous top making it look as though it had been inflated by people breathing Krazy Glue.

Tegel Airport was typically German: quick, efficient, and, for Jeffrey and Rachel, intimidating: There were guards armed with machine guns everywhere they looked.

"You vill be safe . . . or else," Jeffrey muttered as they climbed into a taxi.

"Yes, but with these people you have to wonder who the enemy is," Rachel commented as they drove away. She did not like the idea of coming to Berlin, or even Germany, for that matter. Too much had happened to too many people for her to ever be comfortable. She was the only member of her family ever to return. Her beloved aunt Lena had been the last to leave, minutes ahead of the Jew-hating men sent to take her to a concentration camp. And it was in large part because of Lena, and her legacy, that Rachel now found herself in what she could not but consider enemy territory.

She and Jeffrey had discussed her feelings at length. Jeffrey had made no attempt to dissuade her, but instead pointed out that times, and Germany, had changed. He stressed that the part of Germany they were going to was, in fact, not really German. It was occupied territory, a bastion of the free world smack in the middle of the second world. She had suppressed her feelings, overruled them with her desire to find the man she believed had murdered Henry Thurmond.

Ironically, it was Rachel and not Jeffrey who was the first to capture the excitement of Berlin. Perhaps her jet lag made her more vulnerable, she wasn't sure, but six hours after they had arrived and unpacked, she had begun to sense the energy and excitement of a city that lived as though there were no tomorrow.

They were strolling along the Kurfurstendamm, looking in shop windows, huddled together in the cold. A light snow was falling, yet despite that and the cold the street was crowded. They stopped at a sidewalk counter and bought German sausages sprinkled with spicy mustard and settled into crisp, fresh rolls. They were delicious. They walked several more blocks, and finally went into a store, a big automobile showroom where Jeffrey proceeded to examine the latest-model BMWs. Finally, he looked at his watch and nodded at her. It was time to begin the business that had brought them to Berlin.

They asked the taxi driver to take them to Brandenburg Gate. The driver was surprised to find tourists who wanted to visit the famous gate in the middle of winter. He was even more surprised by their insistence that he not wait for them. He told them twice more they would have difficulty finding a cab so far from the center of the city, but they did not change their minds.

That was what they had been instructed to do.

□□□ **19.** ■

THE TAXI driver, after once again offering to wait, reluctantly let them out at the side of the Reichstag building. Through the thickly wooded forest of barren winter trees, Jeffrey and Rachel could see Brandenburger Tor, and just in front of the towering, regal gate—crossing through the area and immediately behind the Reichstag, the Berlin Wall. They began to walk along the path parallel to the wall.

Because of its wide curve to enclose Brandenburg Gate in the East, they could also see both sides of the wall itself. In the East, it was scrubbed clean and painted white. In the West, it was graffiti-covered, with angry slogans in German and English. RUSSEN RAUS AUS AFGHANIST one said, and immediately below someone had spray-painted—in bright red—POLAND. There were the inevitable love-sick proclamations as well: KERSTIN LOVES CARLOS appeared, a new addition. Another threatened AIDS IN DIE DDR. All the diseases of society, political, sociological, and sexual, were exclaimed in angry scrawls. As if spray paint were a cure, Jeffrey thought to himself.

They kept walking, bending with the path as it wound around the front of the historic gate where the mightiest army in history had once paraded. Machine-gun towers punctuated the wall, square buildings with opaque brown windows, and on the top of each was a railing and a large spotlight. Rachel shivered, and not from the cold. Jeffrey kept his arm linked in hers, pulling her to him. They passed a stately marble statue of a naked warrior whose elbows, shins, and penis had been shot off in the last gasps of war. Across from him was a wooden platform with two short flights of steps leading up to a view of the gate uninterrupted by the wall. Rachel waited while Jeffrey climbed up, pulled his camera out of his pocket, and took a picture. He then turned and, facing Rachel, took a picture of her. He had been told to act like a tourist.

There was snow on the ground and patches of ice along the path. Rachel slipped and Jeffrey grabbed her.

"I don't think they could have chosen a more dra-matic—or remote—spot for the meeting," she muttered.

" 'Remote' is what they said. We wouldn't be inter-rupted. There are very few tourists here at this time of year, and the Reichstag looks absolutely empty. But I'm not sure remote has anything to do with it. I think they want to impress us."

"Then I think I'm impressed."

"Strange what buildings survived the war. Berlin was literally rubble, yet the Reichstag and Brandenburg Gate were still here when it was all over."

They had entered the land of treason. They rounded the last corner of the path before it straightened out to face the towering gate. The forest of trees became even more dense, leading back into the center of the city.

Along the path itself, placed exactly in the center between each tree lining the path, were park benches. On the second bench sat a man, one arm stuffed into his well-cut topcoat, the other holding a cigarette, the smoke from which mingled with the condensation of his breath in the cold air. He was exactly where they had been told he would be, and as they approached he looked up at them and smiled.

"Mr. Dean . . . Miss Sabin?"

He stood to greet them. He was not noticeably tall, but he was very round. They shook hands. He introduced himself as Thebot Cantwell, shooting out his name in short bursts of condensed air as though it would form over his head and remain forever his. "Duty officer of the U.S. Consulate in Berlin," he added, almost as an afterthought. That meant, CIA, though the initials, while understood by all, remained unspoken. "Welcome to Berlin. I have been asked to give you this list."

He reached into his topcoat, extracted an envelope, and from it a single piece of paper. Jeffrey took it and read. Rachel peered over his shoulder. As they read, they both sat down. It was a listing of some fifteen art galleries, plus the names and addresses of two restaurants: Paris Bar and Exile.

"The restaurants are the best-known artists' and dealers' hangouts," Cantwell explained in another burst of cloud.

"And that's where we're to begin asking questions?"

"And in the art galleries too. I have been told all of this was explained to you before you left Los Angeles, but it would be better to go over it all once more. You, Miss Sabin, are a well-connected contemporary-art dealer, one with many wealthy clients, and you are to communicate that the demand has far outstripped the supply as far as you are concerned. You're in the market. You have lots of money.

"You, Mr. Dean," he continued, turning his bulk in Jeffrey's direction, "are to pose as her gallery director, the man responsible for arranging purchases."

Rachel and Jeffrey looked at one another, just as they had two days earlier when the whole thing had first been explained to them in Los Angeles. They nodded.

"If anyone contacts you offering art of the sort you've said you're looking for, let us know immediately. Here's our phone number; it's answered at all hours." He handed them each a small piece of paper with a phone number and his name typed neatly on it. Then he continued.

"I myself do not approve of using civilians in our work. It's dangerous, both for us and for the people we're using. However, I don't make all of the decisions and you're here with us. There will be coverage, which means alternating teams of two men will be watching you at all times."

"Only men?" Rachel asked.

Cantwell ignored her. "If, at any time, you want any of them to approach you, stop briefly, one of you raise your left hand to your right ear. The other does the opposite. Walk for two minutes, then stop again. You will be approached."

"Does this apply when we go across into the East as well?"

"No. You are not to go into the East unless I require it of you. I'll arrange for your coverage to start just after you cross Checkpoint Charlie. You'll be picked up in East Berlin and watched from there.

"Those are my orders. The business of forging art, on the face of it, isn't a political matter. What makes it political is that"—Cantwell nodded his head and two chins in the general direction of the East—"one of their people is involved. One who has apparently put out the lights of a couple of people Stateside."

"That's one way of putting it." Rachel's instincts about Cantwell were troubling her.

"Then, as far as we're concerned, that makes it political. They don't do anything that isn't political."

"If one of these dealers calls with prints which might possibly be the ones we're looking for"—Jeffrey believed in well-laid plans—"we arrange a meeting and let you know right away."

"Correct. Let us know as soon as you can. We'll take it from there."

"You mean we won't be going in to meet the dealer?" Rachel asked.

"Oh, yes you will. It wouldn't work without you. But you'll have plenty of backup. Jesus, it's cold out here."

"You could have chosen a warmer place," Rachel remarked.

"I wanted you to see what it is you're up against. It's a sobering sight."

Jeffrey was right; Cantwell had wanted to impress them. They knew it for certain now.

Cantwell sank farther into his topcoat and adjusted the scarf around his neck. "Look down there," he said, nodding in the general direction of the East and Brandenburg. "Unter den Linden, once a beautiful boulevard, now a run-down collection of buildings selling useless merchandise . . . if you can call political caterwauling 'merchandise.' You know, they've hardly been able to build anything over six stories tall. The damn buildings fall down as fast as they put them up."

"The radio and television tower is much higher than that," Jeffrey tentatively suggested.

"Just like them to put up a symbol which means nothing. It was built to block radio and TV signals from the West, and it isn't all that effective. Berliners call it 'Pope's Revenge.'"

"Why is that?" Rachel asked, looking at the top of the tower sticking up over the highest reaches of Brandenburg Gate, looking almost like a rude interruption in an otherwise polite conversation.

"Look at that big bulge in the middle of it. It's a restaurant. See how the sun strikes it?"

Jeffrey and Rachel looked, and both saw it immediately. The sun formed a cross on the silver covering of the bulge. "Does it always do that?" Rachel asked.

"Always," Cantwell said, his chins and most of his mouth now buried in his scarf. "The tower was built on the site of a bombed-out Catholic church. The nickname stuck."

With that, and with a groan of protest, Cantwell rose. "Keep in touch. We expect a daily report. No problem with the telephones, just call. I'm going to get up and walk back toward the Reichstag. Give me about ten minutes, then you follow."

"Will we have trouble getting a cab out here?" Jeffrey was pounding his hands together, trying to generate warmth from his gloves.

"Shouldn't take too long. Good luck to the both of you. I sure as hell don't understand what Dieter is up to, and I hope we get some answers soon. From the man himself. And he has a lot to answer for. Meanwhile, it's costing an arm and a leg to keep you two at the Steigenberger."

Jeffrey smiled, and Rachel looked down to hide her smile. The Steigenberger—and flying first class—had been his condition. Years as a journalist, traipsing all over the country and abroad, had instilled in him a dislike of any hotel that was not first class. As for the plane tickets, it was an all-night flight and it was his intention they be as comfortable as possible.

They watched Cantwell, whose slight waddle was not nearly so elegant as his tailoring, take the turn on the path leading back to the Reichstag. They waited, Jeffrey stamping his feet and Rachel huddling next to him, and then they set out, stopping at the platform in front of Brandenburg Gate. They stared at the imposing gate, and the gold-winged charioteer at its top facing sightlessly east. Then they continued down the path.

The Reichstag and the large open area in front of it were deserted. They stood, stamping their feet, burying their hands in their pockets, waiting. Finally they walked out and faced the huge old structure. The building looked worn and run down despite its new windows, unable to hide the ravages of history. The engraved symbol at the top of the entry columns read DEM DEUTSCHEN VOLKE.

"Would that it had really been so," Rachel commented.

They waited. After twenty minutes, a light snow began to fall. Still no sign of a taxi, no sign of any sort of transportation.

"How can they be watching us if we're out here in the middle of nowhere and we can't see anyone?" Rachel wondered aloud.

"Let's find out. Raise your right hand to your left earlobe and rub it. I'll use my left."

Minutes later a brown Mercedes pulled around from inside the wooded area and headed in their direction. It came right up to them, stopped, and a man wearing a lined trenchcoat—his right hand reaching into the inside of his jacket—got out.

"Sorry to trouble you," Jeffrey said, smiling. "But it seems we're stuck here and need a ride back to the Steigenberger. Thebot Cantwell said you'd oblige us if we got into a tight spot."

"Jesus," the man said. Then, looking at them and barely concealing his anger, he pulled open the rear door. "Get in."

They rode in silence. As they got out of the car in front of the hotel, the man, looking at his partner first, decided to have the last word.

"He didn't mean that kind of tight spot."

"He wasn't all that specific." Jeffrey smiled back innocently. "And thanks very much."

□□□ 20 ∎

THE NEXT morning they started out. They had the list of galleries Cantwell had given them, and Rachel had called ahead to three of them for appointments. The first gallery occupied a stately prewar building in the Charlottenburg district, one of the city's few relatively intact old neighborhoods, now a hive of gentrification. The gallery itself occupied the ground floor of an old brick building set along a curving street lined with fashionable shops.

"Herr Kimmer, please," Rachel said, taking charge as they'd agreed she would do. "Miss Sabin and Mr. Dean. We have an appointment."

Galerie Kimmer's art was contemporary, a style Rachel categorized as German Neo-Expressionism tailored for a more conservative clientele. They inspected the art and were soon escorted to a spartan office where a large bald man greeted them after he meticulously pulled his shirt cuffs out from beneath his coat sleeves.

Rachel began exactly as she and Jeffrey had rehearsed the night before. She explained that she was a contemporary-art dealer from Los Angeles with a popular gallery. She was, she said, in Europe to expand her contacts and to try to do something about her biggest business problem: an eager, wealthy clientele—not always an expert one at that—and a constant shortage of good commercial art. She concluded by saying she came to Berlin first because of the reputation of its artists and galleries.

"Ah, so you have heard of us," Herr Kimmer said, smiling. "Well then, what can I show you? We have a number of American artists as well."

"Frank Stella is a particularly popular artist in the United States, especially his prints—they're a great deal less expensive than his paintings and equally as popular. Unfortunately there are too few," she said, hoping she wasn't overstating her interest. "Perhaps you have something?"

"Stella? Oh, I'm afraid not. But I have a number of superior artists whose work I'd like to show you."

"That would be good of you," Jeffrey said formally.

There followed two hours of work after work being pulled from storage shelves, unveiled with a flourish and a long explanation. The process always overwhelmed Jeffrey. The smorgasbord of art finally became too much for him to absorb. Rachel's interest usually flagged after the first hour, a time limit she once explained exceeded her judgmental ability. Not this time.

"He has some very good artists," she said as they hailed a cab for their next stop. "I should be so lucky."

"Lucky this time around means finding a murderer."

"We're just beginning," she countered reasonably.

"That's what I'm afraid of."

The next gallery, which turned out to be less than three blocks away in the same neighborhood, was more of the same, except that this time the quality of art was as low as it had been high at the first gallery, and the owner

an overbearing woman who looked, Jeffrey later said, as
though she belonged in a Wagnerian opera.

The weak winter sun was fading early, and clouds
were threatening as they arrived at their final stop for the
day. It was an ornate building with gargoyles everywhere, made historically incongruous by windows that
were thick, contemporary panes set into ancient founda-
tions.

"I thought there wasn't anything left after the war,"
Rachel commented.

"I thought so too. But obviously what little was left
was carefully rebuilt. Or, in this case, overbuilt. My
God, the building looks like a Polish wedding cake."

As they had before entering the two previous
galleries, both turned and looked around to see if they
could spot their guardians, the two people they both assumed would always be in a car not far behind them.
Once again they saw nothing.

Nor did they see anything in the gallery. They were
greeted by an effeminate, overdressed man who, at first,
seemed almost a caricature. He acted infinitely superior to
both Rachel and Jeffrey and as if his art were far superior
to anything they might see in the United States. He as
much as told them so, until Rachel changed her attitude
from businesslike to that of a new convert, desperate for
enlightenment. It worked.

"What shit!" she announced once they had left and
were in a cab on their way back to the Steigenberger.

"Well, he knows where you are," Jeffrey said, "if he's
our man."

"No, my dear," Rachel corrected him archly. "He
knows where you are. I don't think he even noticed me."

"Ah well, I must confess I am a lot more interesting—and a lot better-looking—than the art he was showing us."

Back at the hotel they plunged into the minibar in the room, took off their shoes, rubbed their tired feet, and Jeffrey put in a call to Thebot Cantwell.

"Nothing much to report," he said. "We visited three galleries, and Rachel really made it known she was kind of desperate to buy stuff." Jeffrey paused, listened, then looked up to Rachel's questioning gaze.

"He knows everything we did," he whispered to her, his hand covering the mouthpiece of the telephone. He listened a few more minutes, smiled, and hung up.

"Mr. Cantwell, it turns out, may be a stylish, expensively dressed fat fellow, but he's one cheap civil servant. He would like us to visit four or five galleries tomorrow. Otherwise, at our pace, it's costing the taxpayers too much money."

"That's nothing compared to what dinner is going to cost them," Rachel said, holding up the menu of the Steigenberger's deluxe restaurant.

"Especially when they add on the room-service charge," Jeffrey continued for her. "I'm not budging. I'm going to soak in the bath, order dinner, and read."

"Living well is the best revenge," Rachel said, smiling. "Can I have the bath first?"

"Maybe you'll have to share it."

"Worse things have happened."

□□□21■

THE NEXT day neither the falling snow nor Rachel's falling arches deterred them from their rounds. They were at their first appointment promptly at ten, huddled in the doorway waiting for the gallery owner to appear. Snow was piling up on the street corners and Rachel's feet had gone from sore to sore and cold. Jeffrey, flipping through his Baedeker, discovered KaDeWe, Berlin's massive department store. While Rachel stood undecided before row upon row of boots, he headed for the sixth floor and the food department.

"My God," said Rachel when she joined him later. "This outdoes the food halls at Harrods."

"Even Paul Bocuse has a stand," Jeffrey said, chomping contentedly on a massive salami sandwich and sipping thick black espresso.

"That sounds like something for me."

"He doesn't serve Jewish women in boots."

"Then he'd probably go broke in no time at all," she said, walking away.

Neither could pass up food, and after they had eaten they bought cheese, wine, wafers, and pâté and bundled up for the walk back to the Steigenberger. Rachel's new boots, black leather with fur lining, were perfect. And expensive.

"So what?" Jeffrey said, grinning at her. "We're not paying. Let's head back to the hotel."

Their red message light blinked in the darkness of their room. "Cantwell," Jeffrey said, putting down the phone.

"We'll call him later; otherwise we'll be late for our next great works of art."

"You look this time and after you get started I'll go find a pay phone."

Jeffrey, by now, had some notion of the city itself and had puzzled over the maps before making their appointments. All the afternoon meetings he had arranged were close to one another, all in the city's small but densely populated Indian neighborhood. The sharp smells of curry compounded by a heady mixture of other spices hung in the cold air as they made their way to the first stop. They were less than a block from their destination when a man walked by them, bumped Jeffrey on the shoulder, and said to him, "Call home."

Jeffrey was startled, Rachel amused: "If only your mother could arrange messages like that. You wouldn't be safe anywhere."

"My mother probably could, if she wanted to," Jeffrey added.

The gallery owner was a disheveled, friendly man whose benign nature immediately removed him from their list of suspects. As soon as Rachel was seated and looking at the first of a batch of vigorously colored prints, Jeffrey asked if he could make a telephone call and excused himself.

"It's all arranged," Cantwell told him.

"What is?"

"Tomorrow."

"What tomorrow?"

"The two of you are going to East Berlin."

Jeffrey was silent.

"As tourists. You're going to cross the border, walk in, wander around for a couple of hours to make it all look on the up and up, and then you're going to make a stop."

"What stop?"

"I'll explain later today. What time will you be back at the hotel?"

"By six."

"I'll meet you in the lounge. We'll have a drink."

The rest of the afternoon passed by in a changing maze of prints, paintings, and gallery owners, ranging from interesting to tasteless. Rachel saw little that appealed to her. Jeffrey was beyond making judgments. Both were certain they were making no progress, a condition they both monitored by looking back at the blank stares that greeted them anytime they mentioned Karl Diedrich or Wolfgang Dieter, who for their purposes now became two different people mentioned at different times.

"Six more galleries, and so far as I can tell, nothing," Jeffrey said in the cab on the way back to the hotel.

"At least Thebot will think we're working hard," Rachel countered.

"I expect Thebot likes hard work and results, and one of them he isn't getting." Jeffrey hesitated, then dropped his news. "He's sending us into East Berlin tomorrow."

Rachel greeted this with silence. Jeffrey had anticipated her reaction, and so had waited to tell her later. At the hotel they checked the desk for messages and then

walked across the expansive marble floor into the lounge.
It was a large room, with a bar tucked into one corner, a
grand piano in another, and filled with sofas and padded
chairs facing small tables. A few were occupied. It took
only a second to find Cantwell, seated primly, overflowing a comfortable chair, a teapot and all the ritual china
on a table before him. He was deeply engrossed in the
International Herald Tribune.

"Here's the deal," he said, dispensing with greetings.

"Do I have time to sit down?" Rachel asked sweetly.

Cantwell responded by reaching into his breast pocket
and pulling out an envelope.

"Maps, instructions, everything you'll need."

"That's wonderful, Thebot. Do you mind if we order
first? It's been a busy day." Jeffrey took off his coat and
sat down. Rachel pulled up another chair for their coats.

"So I hear. Six galleries. That leaves six to go, plus
the two restaurants. I figure you won't miss the restaurants."

"You're right. We might even buy everyone a few
rounds of drinks."

"Hmm. Well, if you do, make sure they have information worth buying."

"Look. I know you're not exactly keen on this whole
thing. Neither are we. We're here for our purpose, you're
here for yours. I wish you could submerge your dislike of
this whole thing a little bit so that we can get on with it
and get it over."

"I told you before I don't like civilians doing this sort
of thing. Puts all of us in danger."

"You don't have any choice," Rachel said evenly.
"And at this point neither do we. A very good friend of
ours was murdered by this man. I can recognize him,
maybe even pull him out of his hiding place. That's all.
That's more than I really want to do, except that I want

to do it for a friend, and because I believe crimes should not go unpunished." She was getting angry, and so was Jeffrey.

"When you go across the border tomorrow you'll not just be passing through no-man's-land. You'll be in no-man's-land. I have to see you're protected over there, whatever happens. I don't expect anything will happen, but you never know. I lose a couple of tourists who turn out to be free-lancing for the CIA and I promise you all hell will break loose."

"I sure as hell hope so," Jeffrey said. "Something like that happens, the more pressure on you to get us out, the better."

Cantwell straightened his already perfectly knotted tie and nodded his head. "Let's have a drink. Somehow this tea isn't doing the job."

He waited until the waitress had brought two beers and tea for Rachel before continuing. Then he opened the envelope.

"This is a tourist's map. You can keep it with you. This," he said, handing Jeffrey a single piece of paper, "is your route. Memorize it, or if you must, make yourself some cryptic notes. But don't take this with you. Stick to your instructions exactly, because I'll have people watching you. Every place you're going is on the tourist route. You'll see how really wonderful the People's Republic is. Then you are to find a cab—it won't be easy because there aren't many—and you'll get that by standing outside the entrance to the Palast Hotel. You'll tell the driver to take you to number twenty-two Normannenstrasse. And have him wait."

Cantwell paused. Jeffrey and Rachel committed the instructions to memory.

"It won't take long. Twenty-two Normannenstrasse is the Ministry of State Security. That's where our friend works. You're to walk up to the receptionist's desk—it's in the lobby to your right as you go in—and play tourists to the hilt. Tell the receptionist you met two East Germans at an art gallery in Los Angeles, they told you they were with the East German mission to the U.N., and that you'd like to let them know you're in Berlin."

"Easy," Jeffrey said, making no attempt to hide his doubts.

"If you do it right it will be. Tell them both of his names. And tell them where you're staying. That's all. You can even write out the message, Rachel. That way he'll know it's you. Then you walk out, get back in your taxi, and tell him to take you to Checkpoint Charlie. Get out and walk back across."

"What if he comes right down and greets us?" Rachel asked.

"He won't. No chance. You've got the initiative here. Just leave the message and get the hell out."

Jeffrey felt a tightening in the back of his neck, an obdurate knot of tension. Rachel felt it in her stomach and, had anyone asked, she would have said she would like to get the hell out of Berlin. Right now.

□□□22∎

THEY CROSSED at Friedrichstrasse, Checkpoint Charlie, walking purposefully past the Allied exit point and following the footpath around to the left of the no-man's-land with its red-and-white barriers, where armed Vopos stood guard, their dull green uniforms at first glance unmarked by rank. There was a heavy cloud cover and the checkpoint was virtually empty except for the ever-present Vopos and the seemingly unconcerned small group of American, British, and French soldiers huddled in their small offices.

Once inside the checkpoint, the contrast between East and West was immediately apparent to them both. The East lacked color. The pedestrian building was beige inside and out, with utilitarian tile floors and the smell of disinfectant everywhere. There were no chairs for waiting, no apparent instructions on how to proceed. Jeffrey and Rachel stopped inside the first room, uncertain where to go next. They were confronted by frosted glass inset in a few places on the walls, and a series of doors. It took a minute to overcome the disorientation before Jeffrey saw the small plastic buzzer attached to the wall beside one door. He walked up and pressed it.

The answering buzz startled them both, and they pulled open the door to find themselves in a tiny narrow hall, and to their left a small window with a counter in front of it. A Vopo asked—in German—for their passports. He examined them carefully, looked first at Rachel, checked the photograph again, and then explained, with only a minimal amount of English, that her East German visa would cost five marks, and that she must buy 25 East German marks. She produced the money, was handed her passport, and ordered to proceed. She paused, waiting for Jeffrey. The guard noticed her hesitation and ordered her through the door. She proceeded alone.

Jeffrey joined her a few minutes later, in another antiseptic colorless room, where there was a counter for inspecting luggage and an X-ray machine. This time the Vopo was a woman, who looked them over and then asked to see inside the leather shoulder bag Jeffrey had slung over his shoulder. He emptied the contents on the counter. The guard looked through the tourist map, the guidebook, glanced at his camera, and then said they could proceed.

They walked through another narrow hall, which smelled even more strongly of disinfectant and out another door to find themselves outside in a walkway between two high cement walls. They continued on their way, turned left at the end, and found themselves at the eastern end of Checkpoint Charlie, standing before a metal-bar gate. They stood for a minute before a Vopo came out of one of the guard shacks, walked across the passenger-car inspection area, and opened the gate for them. They were now in East Berlin.

"Jesus," Jeffrey muttered under his breath as they began picking their way through the rubble of construction that surrounded the gate.

"If I didn't know better, I'd think they were on to us," Rachel said quietly.

"I feel the same. But it's that way for everyone going through. Here's the map—you navigate."

Navigation was easy; negotiating the broken sidewalks and rubble was not. They were on Glinkastrasse walking toward Unter den Linden, the great boulevard of the Berlin that once was. There were few pedestrians and even fewer cars on the street. What few there were were asthmatic-sounding Skodas and Ladas. The western roar of traffic and the off-key symphony of horns was completely absent. They walked by the Comic Opera and arrived on the broad boulevard itself.

"I feel like I've stepped through Alice's looking glass," Rachel said. "Everything's suddenly turned around." They stood looking down Unter den Linden toward the Brandenburg Gate, which was exactly as they'd seen it from the west, except that this time the winged charioteer was facing in their direction. They walked toward the gate, along East Berlin's embassy row, past the Polish, Soviet, and Hungarian embassies. They paused, and Jeffrey took out his camera. Cantwell had been specific: Take your camera and take lots of touristy pictures.

"Look like a tourist," he instructed her. An East Berliner walked past them and smiled. Jeffrey held out the camera and the elderly woman smiled again, and took their picture.

Then they turned and headed back toward the center of the city. The linden trees that gave the boulevard its name were barren, and so were all the other trees lining the broad avenue.

"This is damned depressing," Jeffrey said as they headed toward the National Library and the Tomb of the Unknown Soldier.

"Imagine what it must be like to live here," Rachel said. "And to know all the time that the decadent West is just a few yards away. Are we on schedule?"

Jeffrey glanced at his wristwatch. It was 11 A.M. "Pretty much so. Let's go check out the anonymous dead."

It was a small building compared to the massive structures fronting the boulevard, and it looked more like a Greek temple than a memorial. Armed guards stood rigidly at attention as Jeffrey and Rachel passed the entry columns and walked into the small marble room. One wall was engraved, and Rachel read it aloud, translating as she went: "To the Victims of Fascism and Militarism." In the center of the room was a crystal cube reflecting the eternal flame burning beneath it. Along the walls were small banners and bunches of flowers. Jeffrey walked over to look at them.

"They're plastic," he said to her. "I guess that makes it easy to replenish them. Next?"

"The television tower and a cup of coffee."

They proceeded down Unter den Linden and on through Marx-Engels-Platz past the Foreign Ministry, with its rows of brown-tinted windows and empty plaza. Ahead of them, in sharp contrast to the stark modernity of the Foreign Ministry, was the Old Museum and the great dome of the Berlin Cathedral. Farther ahead they could see the television tower looming over the city. It took nearly fifteen minutes to walk to it, and they arrived cold and hungry. The elevator ride to the building's restaurant, the giant glass bubble near its top, made them both feel claustrophobic and uneasy. The restaurant itself was spartan and there were few customers. Jeffrey paused at a display case of pastries.

"I figure they can do whatever they want with people here," he said after they were seated, "but I'll bet there's no way in the world you're going to stop these people from making the best pastries in the world."

He was right. They drank rich, dark coffee and ate rich, dark pastries. They were both tense and quiet, unwilling to speak their thoughts, as though to do so might make them public. Rachel broke the uneasy silence.

"I don't understand how they can be watching us. There isn't enough traffic and there aren't enough people around."

"They know our route. That's why Cantwell told us exactly where to go."

"Still, I wonder."

"Do you leave tips?" Jeffrey was examining the bill.

"You're not supposed to."

"What the hell. We're tourists. And I bet the waitress isn't about to refuse money."

He was right. He took the heavy brass coat check from his pocket, tipped again at the cloakroom, and they left, walking briskly the short distance back up the Unter den Linden to the Palast Hotel, a modern mass of concrete and more beige-tinted windows facing the boulevard. The entrance, however, was in the back, so they walked to the revolving doors and found themselves standing alone, looking anxiously down an empty—except for very few parked cars—driveway. Eventually a man approached whom Jeffrey assumed from his dress—a sort of nondescript uniform—worked for the hotel.

"Can I get a taxi here?"

The man looked at him and, with his index finger pointing at the cement at his feet, gestured for him to wait.

"Talkative, these East Berliners," Jeffrey said as the man left. Rachel stood in the warmth of the lobby while Jeffrey waited. It ended up being nearly fifteen minutes until they entered the taxi, and by then they were almost half an hour behind schedule.

He had prepared himself. On a small piece of paper he had written the address 22 Normannenstrasse, and from his phrase book the words for "please wait" in German.

"Very clever," Rachel said, smiling uneasily at him. The taxi was, like all the cars they saw in East Berlin, of a make unfamiliar to them both, small cars that gave out a sort of whine and quite a bit of exhaust. The ride took less than ten minutes.

They found themselves facing another modern brown building, this one some seven stories tall with bank upon bank of beige windows that reflected the small amount of sunlight peering through the clouds. They walked quickly to the center door and across the marble lobby to the reception desk, which, as Cantwell had promised, was to their right.

"Excuse me," Jeffrey said politely. "I'm here to inquire about a friend. Someone we met at home. Home," he added with a smile he thought must immediately betray his tension, "is Los Angeles."

"We're from California," Rachel chimed in.

The receptionist gave them an uncomprehending look.

"We met two fellows in Los Angeles who were with the cultural-affairs office of the U.N."

"That's in New York," Rachel interrupted.

The receptionist was a stern-looking woman in her mid-fifties who was not accustomed to tourists. Comprehension came slowly.

"Their names?" she finally asked in measured English.

"Karl Diedrich and Wolfgang Dieter," Jeffrey immediately replied. "They said they were from East Berlin."

"With State Security?" she asked.

The question—an obvious one—wasn't something they had prepared for. They hesitated until Jeffrey tumbled into a speech, one he created as he went along.

"I'm not sure. You see"—he paused and looked at Rachel as if she might somehow silently provide him with the correct answer—"we don't know your government . . . or how it works."

"Did you try the Foreign Ministry?"

"Yes," Rachel lied. "But we thought we'd come here too. Never hurts to leave your name around. They were very nice men and we thought it would be so nice to see them again. You see, we are all interested in art."

"Write their names, please," the woman said, handing them a piece of paper and a pen from the drawer of her desk.

Jeffrey wrote both names, then added the name of their hotel. "That's where they can find us," he said, attempting another smile.

As he spoke, the woman pressed a button on the frame of her desk near her lap. A video camera—Rachel had noticed three of them scanning the lobby as they entered—focused on their faces and recorded their images on videotape.

"Thank you for inquiring," the woman said at them without smiling. "I will attempt to locate them. I doubt they are with State Security, but we shall see."

Indeed we shall, Rachel thought. They thanked the woman and Jeffrey, unable to resist the urge, looked about the sterile, cold lobby and said, "Nice building you have here."

The woman, knowing better, said, "Thank you."

The taxi was waiting, and they instructed the driver

to take them to Checkpoint Charlie, and when they were within a block of the border the driver pulled to the curb and motioned them out. Jeffrey paid, adding on a large tip, and they began once again to pick their way through the construction sites and rubble, along the broken and uneven sidewalk, to the checkpoint. This time there was a line of ten people before them, none in the drab clothing that marked East Berliners. Westerners were leaving; East Germans could not. It took over an hour to cross the border. They retraced their earlier steps exactly. After going through the iron gate and down the walk, they noticed a foot scraper with stubs for brushes as they entered the building. Jeffrey scraped his feet, Rachel smiling at him. In the first room Jeffrey placed his shoulder bag on the counter once again.

"Money?" the guard asked.

"None," Jeffrey said. He had given the last of their East German marks to the taxi driver. The guard—it was a young man this time, so young his blond beard appeared virtually nonexistent except for a few determined hairs sticking out from his chin—carefully examined their passports. They returned to the tiny enclosed hallway with the Vopo still sitting at the window. There was room for three people in the hall, and when they entered there were eight people packed shoulder to shoulder in it. Eventually they reached the Vopo and handed him their passports. He looked them over carefully, peering closely at Rachel and Jeffrey and then above their heads. Jeffrey could see, in the reflection of the guard's glasses, another mirror, directly behind him.

"You may go," the guard said. As they walked out of the hall and into the small room leading to the Allied side of the border, Jeffrey noticed the man close the window and heard the sigh of those still waiting in line. The Vopo turned from his desk to his telephone, and dialed extension 59—the Ministry of State Security.

"The two people you asked about have crossed. I let them go as you ordered," he said. He looked down at his wristwatch, preparing himself in case there were to be questions later. It was 1 P.M.

□□□ 23 ∎

A LIGHT rain mixed with snow began falling as they walked back into the Allied sector of the checkpoint, their heads down against the steady wind, their feet crunching the dirt and sand that had been scattered on the ground by the footsteps of those who had gone before them. To their left they saw the wooden platform placed so that Westerners could look over the wall and take photographs of the border. And, just ahead of them on Friedrichstrasse, in a new building painted white and gray, HAUS AM CHECKPOINT CHARLIE, the museum of politics, Berlin style.

"I want some hot coffee. And something to eat." Rachel wanted food and a warm place to sit.

The entrance to the museum contained a small coffee shop, and within minutes they had shed their winter coverings and were sitting comfortably in the plastic chairs, sipping coffee and eating pastries. They did not speak, and were alone with their thoughts of the East when Thebot Cantwell waddled in, took off his camel's hair coat, and joined the line at the coffee counter.

"Well, how did it go?" he asked as he sat down.

"Fine," Jeffrey said. "Just fine." Cantwell provoked his curiosity, but Jeffrey restrained himself.

"That's all you've got to say?"

"It came off exactly as you planned it. No hitches, nothing. Now what?"

"We wait to hear from your friend Wolfgang Dieter."

"Waiting is kind of expensive, isn't it?"

"Not when there's a payoff. And not if it doesn't last too long."

Jeffrey wondered why Cantwell, who went to considerable trouble to remind them how busy he was, came to Checkpoint Charlie to get such a simple report. One that could easily have been telephoned to him. His instinct, in the form of a peripheral thought that sped across the back of his mind and then disappeared quickly, told him something more was at stake. Cantwell interrupted his musing.

"We'll need you to go back once, maybe twice, more. We want to get his attention, worry him a little. And get him looking for you. The ideal thing would be if Dieter turned up . . . on this side of the wall."

"And then. . . ?" Rachel asked.

"We ask him a few questions. Or, rather, you do."

"Want to give them to us now?"

"Later. My people . . ." Cantwell raised his left hand and pointed in the general direction of the center of the city, as though he had at his command a building full of busy workers. "My people are getting something ready."

Jeffrey was beginning to feel out of place. And he was getting suspicious. Cantwell was too watchful, his dark eyes didn't waver, and his manner did not permit understanding.

"You'll ask him some questions," Cantwell repeated. "Then you'll lead him to us. As soon as he contacts you, we'll know it."

"I hope so." Rachel shivered at the thought of the two of them alone with a man they both were certain was a murderer.

"Have you had a look around the museum?" Cantwell smiled evenly. "You must. It's absolutely amazing what lengths people will go to to get to our side of the wall."

With a dismissive "We'll be in touch," he left them, left them feeling uneasy and uncertain about what was to come next. They draped their heavy coats over their arms and began walking through the small, labyrinthine museum, examining the collection of escape routes used to get out of East Berlin. Rachel wondered what she'd give up to escape from both Berlins.

They found a hot-air balloon, a bullet-riddled car with a hiding place built into its reinforced interior, a bicycle, home-made scuba gear, a high wire, and two suitcases formed together to hide one person. Beside each exhibit were photographs of the escape routes, and maps of the city. There were also photographs of the building of the wall, the Berlin airlift, and the piles of rubble that constituted Berlin at the end of the war. Another series of rooms displayed protest art, passionate but not necessarily well-painted works featuring a gallery of political protesters from Gandhi on to black South Africans. Because the museum wandered from the new building into an older, smaller building next door, the exhibit rooms became progressively smaller until they found themselves looking at tunnels in what seemed like a tunnel, and the effect made them both claustrophobic.

"What? No Picasso? No *Guernica*?" Jeffrey said as they reached the small museum store, where postcard and poster reproductions of much of the exhibit were on sale.

Jeffrey selected a T-shirt emblazoned with a reproduction of Checkpoint Charlie to give to Michael. Rachel handed it back for a larger size, and Jeffrey was struck

with the realization that he and his fourteen-year-old son
wore the same size now. Rachel bought Michael a minia-
ture Brandenberg Gate.

At the corner outside the museum they looked back at
the checkpoint, then, without comment and at first each
unaware the other was doing it, they both looked about
to spot their tail. Jeffrey saw Rachel looking.

"In that collection of Mercedeses and BMW's out
there, one of them is watching us."

"And that Mercedes there," Rachel added, pointing at
the taxi queue, "is waiting for us. I'm freezing."

There were two messages for them back at the hotel,
both from art dealers eager to make a sale. In their room
they found a bowl of fresh fruit from the hotel manager,
and under it a guide map to Berlin. Jeffrey sat down and
began looking at it. Rachel struggled out of her boots.

"Did you feel fear when we were over there?"

"Yes, yes of course," she replied. "And I was struck
by the absolute lack of color. I'd always associated bright
colors with the East, I guess because of their flags and
banners. But nothing, nothing at all. Even their clothing.
It's depressing."

"Imagine what it's like to live there."

"They call it 'the City of Peace.'"

"Yes, and they call us the principal enemy."

"Do you think Dieter will turn up?"

"Yes."

"You sound certain."

"Nearly. It's something I feel. It's not preordained,
but it's almost as though it's prearranged. I don't mean
we're being set up, but it's almost like that."

Rachel walked into the bathroom. She soon reappeared in her robe and began hanging her clothing in the
closet. "Were *you* afraid?"

"Yes, a little," he answered her. "But my tendency is

minute or two later he stirred, and she reached out to him, began caressing the hair on his chest, circling a finger idly around his nipples.

"Can I do that to you?" he asked sleepily.

"And more, I hope," she said as she leaned over to kiss him.

His hand found her breasts, and soon his lips took its place. Their lovemaking was now one of habit, for each knew the other well, knew how to please and excite. Jeffrey, more than Rachel, was a creature of habit. She once explained to him that she experimented with variety because she was afraid of his losing interest in her. She slid under the covers and he felt her tongue retrace the route of her fingers until he moaned with pleasure.

"I'm not going to last long if you keep that up," he whispered.

"You're the one who has to keep it up," she giggled.

"Right now, no problem. No problem at all."

Two hours later they were dressed and ready for dinner. Jeffrey had made reservations at the Paris Bar, one of the restaurants mentioned by Cantwell. It was less than five minutes by taxi from their hotel, and they were ready early.

They decided to stop in the hotel's bar and have a drink, to watch other guests and enjoy the comfort of the room. Rachel's heels clicked as she walked across the marble lobby and Jeffrey noticed several men looking at her. He too joined the spectators briefly, and was once again struck by her presence. She was wearing a black wool sweater dress, her long black hair falling about her shoulders. She wore the strand of pearls Lena had left her, and a small diamond ring on her right hand, a ring she once told him signified to her that she was taken— not married, but taken.

to suppress my feelings at times like that and to concentrate on what has to be done. I guess it's a way of dealing with what I feel. Kind of like going to the dentist. I am afraid of dentists, I have been all my life, and I remember as a child going into the waiting room and then focusing all my attention on a story in a magazine. My concentration helped me to escape my emotions."

"Is that why you started reading that map as soon as we got to the room?"

"Probably. I hadn't thought of it that way, but yes. And I do it with books, I always have. Right now it's this." He held up a paperback copy of John le Carré's *The Spy Who Came in from the Cold.*

"A novel about a man who is killed crossing the Berlin Wall?"

"Yes. Do you know what a first edition of this book is worth?"

"No. With or without an inscription from le Carré?"

"Rough estimate: three hundred dollars for a British first edition, three seventy-five inscribed."

"Le Carré's inscription is worth seventy-five dollars?"

"On one of his earlier books in the British edition, yes. The later books, with inscription, would sell for less. He's very much alive and still writing."

"Lucky him."

"Lucky me."

She laughed. "Whatever turns you on, Jeffrey."

"You know what turns me on." He looked at her, put down his book, and reached out to her.

"Not until I've had my bath." She closed the bathroom door, and he could hear the water running. He removed his clothes and climbed into the bed, intending to wait. She spent longer than usual in the bathroom, and when she came out he was asleep, snoring lightly. She slid into bed beside him, taking care not to wake him. A

They were at the entrance to the lounge when the man made his approach. He was in his sixties, slightly stooped. His English was heavily accented.

"Miss Sabin, Mr. Dean. I am told you are looking for some prints by Frank Stella."

They were rooted in place, and said nothing. It was, Rachel thought later, as if they had suddenly become a living tableau. The man continued.

"My name is Steiner. I have two prints which I would like to show you."

"Perhaps we can make an appointment for tomorrow?"

"That is not possible. You must come with me now."

"How did you know us?" Rachel asked.

"I followed you yesterday. At the galleries. I heard what you were looking for from someone I know at a gallery. It is not a big world, the art galleries."

"I see. Where are the prints?"

"Nearby. If you will come with me now, you can look at them. Have you traveler's checks or cash?"

"Yes," Jeffrey said, feeling for his wallet, making certain he hadn't left it in their room. He was willing, though he was also aware Rachel had stepped back slightly, undecided.

"Come with me, please." He turned toward the lounge.

"The door is this way," Rachel corrected him.

"So are the men who are following you. I know another way."

He led them into the lounge and across the large room to a door along a wall filled with photographs of celebrities who had stayed at the hotel. They went through the door and down a long hallway. Finally, he opened another door. They were in a shop, one of the many small boutiques that lined the side street leading to the hotel.

This one was filled with samovars of every size and description. Rachel and Jeffrey remembered seeing it from the street.

The shopkeeper glanced up briefly. The man nodded at her and she quickly turned her back as they walked through the store and out onto the street.

"Look at this, please," he said, stepping into a dark doorway before they reached the busy corner. Rachel and Jeffrey looked and saw he had a gun pointed at them.

"I do not want to use it. But I will if there is trouble. Walk ahead of me. We are only going a short distance."

"Don't be stupid," Jeffrey shot back at him. "We are only art dealers. We do not do business this way."

"Mr. Dean," the man said, with an air of resignation and, it seemed, infinite patience. "I know what you are looking for. I also know who you are looking for."

□□□ 24 ∎

IT WAS a shabby, cramped pension less than two blocks away. Steiner motioned them ahead up four flights of stairs without a word, hardly pausing to catch his breath although he was obviously winded from the climb.

"Here we are. Make comfortable, please."

They both stood in the center of the room, not even removing their coats.

"I will not harm you. Take your coat off please. Both."

As they did, Steiner stepped to a wardrobe closet, swung open the door and pulled a large tube out. He sat it on the bed and then removed his coat and carefully hung it in the closet. Jeffrey could see he had only the clothes he wore, nothing more. He could also see that the gun went into the closet along with the coat.

It was a shot in the dark, but Jeffrey decided it was worth a try. "How do you get across the border so easily, Herr Steiner?"

"I have a passport," he said, smiling. "Swiss."

"Forged?"

"Of course." And this time the smile was even wider. "Here they are," he said, rolling the two prints out on the bed. The colorless room burst to life. Both prints were from Stella's *Had Gadya,* and both were blessed with color, lots of it.

Rachel knelt beside the bed, which the Stellas covered, almost as if she were saying her prayers. She inspected them carefully, and could find no hint of forgery. She also knew she was woefully inadequate at detecting that sort of thing. She looked some more, then glanced at Jeffrey and shrugged.

"These, of course, are forgeries." Jeffrey felt he had absolutely nothing to lose.

"Yes, but very good, don't you think?" Steiner's pride was obvious.

"You did them?" Rachel asked.

"Most."

"How many of you are there?"

"Three," Steiner smiled again. "I think you find customers easy, yes?"

"Oh yes," Rachel agreed. She was just beginning to realize how easy it could be. It was against everything she stood for, but she was nevertheless capable of imagining the money to be made. She smiled. "How much?"

"Here. I've figured it out in dollars." Steiner reached inside his suit coat, which was shiny and worn but spotlessly clean, and pulled out a piece of paper. "Three thousand dollars each. A good price, yes?"

"Oh yes," Jeffrey agreed. "Are there more?"

"Perhaps."

"Where were they printed?"

"In the East." Steiner emphasized the information by pointing in the direction of East Berlin. "You ask many questions, Mr. Dean."

"I need many answers, Herr Steiner."

"Why is that so?"

"To make sure it is safe to do business with you."

"Oh, it is safe. With me."

"How did you hear of us?" Rachel was starting through her list of rapidly forming questions.

"At the print shop. They said that the two Americans had come to Berlin looking for Stellas."

Jeffrey suddenly understood. It was all beginning to fit together. Steiner was—comparatively speaking—an innocent. He was a master forger, no more, no less. And now he was trying to make money on the side, unaware of the consequences. He had no idea he was involved with a murderer.

"Who is 'they'?" This time, Jeffrey's question was tentative.

"The two men who pay us and sell the prints."

"Who are they?"

"That I don't tell. Too . . . what is the word?"

"Risky?" Rachel was figuring it out too.

"Ja. Risky. They don't know about these," Steiner said, looking down at the two Stellas. "You must not tell them."

"We won't," Rachel promised. "Would they be angry if they knew about what you were doing?"

"Oh. Ja. Very angry."

"Why are you taking such a chance?" Jeffrey had a theory, but he wanted to prove it.

"I have Swiss passport, yes? And almost money to go and live in Switzerland. There"—his head moved in the direction of the East—"I am criminal. Out of prison, but watched. I have no future."

Jeffrey reached for his wallet, and counted out $3,000 in traveler's checks. "I have only enough money for one.

Tomorrow I will get more money. Can you meet me tomorrow?"

"Perhaps. But I will accept only . . . real money."

"That's not possible right now. I don't carry that kind of money in my pocket."

Steiner slowly deflated, a look of abject disappointment replacing his ready smile. "Always complications."

"Always," Rachel said. She even felt a bit sorry about disappointing him. "We promise you, we will have the money tomorrow."

"Tomorrow, maybe. I will contact you. Be very careful. The men say you are followed everywhere. Do you know that?"

Rachel and Jeffrey nodded.

"Then, when the time comes, go out of the hotel as I took you. Just give the shopkeeper a few marks. She understands."

"Why?"

"Why not?" Steiner's smile was back again. "This is Berlin. It happens all of the time. Now you must go."

Jeffrey had one last question. "Herr Steiner, you said you knew the man we were looking for. Is it Wolfgang Dieter?"

"No, that is not the name. No more questions. You must go now. Please hurry." He handed them their coats, and helped Rachel into hers. Without another word, he showed them to the door, and they heard the double lock turn as they started down the dark stairway.

As soon as they were on the street, Jeffrey stopped. "Go call Cantwell. Tell him where we are and what has happened. Hurry. I'll wait here in case he leaves."

"What if he does?"

"I'll follow him."

"I don't think that's a good idea."

"Rachel, there isn't time. Quickly, call Cantwell. Let him do it for us."

She left, and within a block he could see her turn into a drugstore, searching in her purse for change. He stepped into the doorway of a shop selling Braun equipment, and pretended to be looking at alarm clocks and shavers. He kept the door to the pension in sight at all times, and was about to begin an inspection of coffee makers when he remembered reading once that professional followers used reversible jackets and reversible hats so that they could quickly change disguise. He looked down at his Burberry. No way, he thought. I'd look like a racehorse.

He checked his watch. It was ten minutes after eight. He looked up in gratitude at the outdoor heater warming the entrance to the store. Then he glanced again at the pension. Steiner, the tube with the two Stellas hooked under his left arm, walked out the door, glanced both ways along the boulevard, and started off in the opposite direction. Jeffrey quickly stepped out onto the street and looked for Rachel. If she was coming, she'd be passing directly by Steiner. He could not see her. He hesitated briefly, then quickly began to follow his man.

□□□ 25 ■

WITHIN TWO blocks, Jeffrey guessed where Steiner was
going. The old man moved with the agility and speed of
a frightened rabbit, maneuvering easily around other pedestrians, unfazed by obstacles, and not in the least ham-
pered by the big cardboard tube, which he now carried
vertically, clutched to his chest. Because the tube was
long, and Steiner short, it provided a sort of signal for
Jeffrey. He could see the tube at all times, but he seldom
caught sight of Steiner himself.

Jeffrey was right. He watched the tube bob into the
U-Bahn station in the center of a crowd of people. Jeffrey
dodged and weaved his way into the station, clattered
down the stairs, bought his ticket, then joined a group of
three other men waiting for a train. Steiner was at the
other end of the platform. He looked around him several
times, and when he did Jeffrey hunched his shoulders,
pulled his hat down, and turned away from him. When
the train rolled into the station, Jeffrey waited. He hoped
not too long, because timing was critical. His instinct

told him when the doors were about to slide shut, and he ran past three cars and jumped into the last door of the car behind Steiner's. The train was crowded, and as he inched his way toward Steiner he studied the map. Three stops to the Zoo Station, where he assumed Steiner would change trains for the Friedrichstrasse train bound for East Berlin. He had Steiner—or rather the tube—in sight before the first stop.

At the Zoo Station, the crowd was even larger. Jeffrey's height made it possible to see over the crowd and never lose sight of the round cardboard homing beacon bobbing along some thirty feet ahead of him. It was working perfectly and he was certain he could follow him all the way to the U-Bahn checkpoint. He was equally certain he would be spotted the moment he lined up at the border crossing as Steiner reentered the East. He boarded the train, taking care to be only one car behind Steiner. This time he could not see the tube—Steiner must have set it down. There was plenty of room, the train virtually empty. Only four other passengers were in Jeffrey's coach. He was soon sweating, as much from anxiety as from the warm winter clothes inside a warm train. Three stops to go.

He watched the others as they left the train. He was struck by the fact that even animated conversations stopped as the line formed at the control point. Some might cross frequently, others almost daily, but it nevertheless was a solemn occasion. Politics, Jeffrey thought, not only makes strange bedfellows, it makes the bedfellows uncomfortable. Steiner was at the head of the line, fumbling in his pocket—Jeffrey assumed he was looking for his Swiss passport—unaware of those behind him. Jeffrey stood with his back to the wall, sliding down slightly and turned a bit away, just five people behind his quarry. This was not going to work, he was certain of it.

Steiner passed through, and Jeffrey knew his head start would make it impossible to catch up. Still, he was willing to give it a try. Jeffrey showed his passport, bought his East German marks, paid for his visa, and walked through to the inspection room. He was ordered to go directly through it because he had no packages. As he walked along the edge of the room toward the door, he passed within inches of Steiner's back. Steiner was talking in adamant German, waving a clutch of papers, as the Vopo, his machine gun slung haphazardly on his shoulder, stood puzzling over the two Stellas, which were unwrapped and lying on the counter. Another Vopo held out his hands for Steiner's papers—Jeffrey guessed they were documents for carrying the package—as another border crosser bumped into Jeffrey from behind.

He found an unoccupied doorway near the border and waited, rubbing his hands and stamping his feet to keep warm. Fifteen minutes later Steiner, his tube once again bobbing before him, emerged. This time Jeffrey lengthened the distance between them. There were few pedestrians. In the distance he could see into West Berlin, where lights in buildings and on the streets burned brightly. In the East, there were few lights, and the street lighting was dim. He was in another section of the city, but it was in a different world.

In two blocks, Steiner halted, leaned his package against a bus stop, and waited. Jeffrey halted also, swearing to himself. If Steiner got on a bus, there was no possible way Jeffrey could get on the same one. He began to panic, took a deep breath, and looked around him. There was a bicycle rack up against one side wall, and there were bicycles in it. Five of them. He checked them all, and every one was bound by chain and lock to the rack. Across the street, in the opposite direction from Steiner, Jeffrey saw a bar, its neon sign flashing dimly in the night. Beside the bar was a side wall, an alley of some sort, and he could see another bicycle rack. He willed himself to walk casually across the street. There was hardly any traffic, and he had no sooner stepped off the curb than he noticed a bus approaching less than a block away. He looked around and saw Steiner gather up his package. This was it.

There were more bicycles this time, and Jeffrey didn't take the time to inspect them. He just pulled the first one off the rack, and let go of it as soon as the chain resisted. The fifth bicycle he pulled came out. He looked quickly around: No one had seen him. The bus had already passed, and when he rode out onto the street, he could see it was at least two blocks ahead of him. He pushed hard and swore. The bicycle was old, unreliable, unsteady, and unwilling. He pushed harder, but could gain little on the bus.

He was wet with sweat in less than ten minutes, but he had made up some ground. The wheels were bent with age, and he thought he must look like a drunk on a bike, but he kept pushing. He stopped pedaling only when he could feel his hat begin to slip from his head. After two perilous attempts to remove one hand from the handlebars, he pulled off his hat, put the brim between his teeth and kept going.

He guessed he had pedaled fifteen minutes or more when he saw the bus stop and the familiar tube go around a corner down a side street. To his right he could see the Spree, and the various warehouses and industrial sites along the waterfront. That's where Steiner was heading. He pedaled furiously, turned perilously around the corner. Steiner was two blocks ahead, walking directly toward the river. Jeffrey slowed.

The tube and Steiner entered an old warehouse one building away from the riverfront. Jeffrey saw him lean the tube against a wall, pull keys out of his pocket, open two locks, then enter the building. He did not see any lights come on. In the silence of the abandoned side street, the bicycle's screeching and scraping brought him to a frightened halt. Jeffrey got off, wheeled it into a dark doorway, and proceeded on foot. He put his hat back on. At the corner by the building he stopped. Which would be better, going straight for the door or turning at the side of the building and looking for a window to peer in? He was debating when the flash of car headlights turning onto the street forced him to move, move away from the street and along the side of the building. He darted across the street and crouched down alongside a trash bin as the car pulled up in front of the building and stopped by the door Steiner had entered less than two minutes earlier. Jeffrey crept from the trash bin—his legs were beginning to ache already—across the narrow street to the building. At the side opposite the door, he saw windows and, cutting through the darkness, a beam of light from inside.

The warehouse window was too high for easy access, so Jeffrey was confronted with the prospect of climbing onto the large oilcan that sat beneath it, and risking noise. He slipped off his shoes and pulled himself to the top of the barrel. He found himself standing in his stocking feet on a barrel rim full of frozen water. He slipped his shoes back on, using the edge of the wall next to the window for balance. Then he looked.

Steiner was not alone. A man of medium height, with thinning blond hair and sunken cheeks was facing him, gesturing wildly with his arms. It was obvious Steiner was in trouble. His hands faced the other man, palms out, defensively. The stranger was shouting, and Steiner answered in a halting voice. Jeffrey raised himself higher. He saw each man from the side, so it was unlikely either would see him. The confrontation went on, and Jeffrey began to hear, but he could not understand German. There was an elaborate state-of-the-art printer in the room, along with a large marble-topped work table.

This was the place. Another Stella, one from the pro-tractor series, was partially printed, waiting for comple-tion on the big press. Others, in various stages of completion, rested on the marble.

Jeffrey had seen enough, and was about to leave when he heard the man shout at Steiner.

"Sabin und Dean" was what he heard, and all that he needed to hear. He also saw Steiner's affirmative nod. The man pulled a gun from his topcoat. Jeffrey ducked out of sight, but he could still hear Steiner pleading. When he heard a soft thud, he knew it was the silencer on the gun smothering the sound.

He looked once again. Steiner's body was on the ce-ment floor. He had been shot in the forehead. The man was unrolling a large canvas tarp. Jeffrey watched as he rolled Steiner's body onto the tarp, secured it around him, and then moved two large cans to either end of the bundle. He knew they were heavy, because he saw the man's face color as he lifted them.

Steiner, he was certain, was destined for the bottom of the Spree. He took off his shoes once again and jumped off the top of the barrel. He did not pause to put them on, but ran to the large trash bin where he had hid-den before, and crouched down to put them on there. He ran for the bicycle and began pedaling his way back to the Freidrichstrasse U-Bahn station.

He carefully retraced his route and within half an hour found he was on Unter den Linden, and he could see the rubble leading to Checkpoint Charlie. He decided to cross there, in case the same guard at the U-Bahn check-

point was still on duty. Jeffrey placed the bicycle against
the wall of the Russian tourist office, a nondescript building whose windows were full of photographs of reapers
harvesting wheat.

It was just past midnight. He started out for Checkpoint Charlie.

□□□ 26 ∎

HE FOUND her in the hotel lounge, sitting on a couch sipping tea. Her face was as pale as the faded pink couch. Next to her, overflowing a capacious chair, a cigar stuck grimly in his mouth, was Theo Cantwell. He looked at them for a moment before they saw him. Rachel stood, the relief on her face a measure of how much she cared for him. He liked that. Cantwell, on the other hand, just shook his head. In a matter of seconds Jeffrey went from feeling like a hero to comprehending he was a wayward, bad boy. He immediately went on the defensive.

"I followed Steiner. He led me to the printers. I know where the forgeries are made, Rachel."

"What about Dieter?" Cantwell was all business.

Jeffrey ignored him. He sat down, ordered a double brandy, stretched his aching legs, and told his story.

"He was murdered?" Rachel couldn't quite comprehend what he had seen.

"Yes. And I think for contacting us. I heard your name and mine. That's all I understood."

"Oh, God."

"I told you not to go off by yourselves." Cantwell tried to contain—with not much success—his anger.

"What choice did I have? You wanted information, now you've got it."

"I want Dieter. Not some goddamned forgery factory."

Jeffrey's instinct immediately alerted him that they were at cross purposes, and had always been. Now he could be certain of it. But his fatigue moderated his instinct. He was not at this moment given to reason, but he tried nevertheless.

"I believe you said earlier that if you find one, you will likely find the other."

"You found it. And you didn't find the other." Cantwell impatiently relit his cigar.

"Maybe I will." Jeffrey stiffened in his chair.

Cantwell said nothing, but his grunt of dismissal caused at least two of his chins to shake.

"We know a lot now. And I suspect we can learn more." Rachel was so relieved to see Jeffrey, she made a mistaken attempt to apply reason where, at this moment, nothing would stick.

"You suspect." Cantwell's comment was withering.

"I suspect something too. You want to hear what it is, Theo?" Jeffrey sipped his brandy, and did not wait for Cantwell to respond. "Here it is. You don't give a hoot in hell about the murder that brought us here, the art forgeries, the whole rotten business. It's beneath you. You want only one thing. You want Dieter. And you're using us for just one reason: to get him."

"Well, well. So that's why you followed Steiner. You have the true missionary zeal of the committed. You really know what you want. I, on the other hand, want something else. You're quite right there, by the way. I advised against your being sent over here. I didn't want anything to do with it. I still don't. But there is one thing about it all that appeals to me, and you hit it right on the mark. You may lead me to Dieter. That's what I want, that's what I'm here to get, and I'm going to get it." Cantwell leaned forward for emphasis, seemingly unencumbered by his girth. "Get it, that is, one way or another."

"Is that a threat?"

"Of a sort. You're here against my wishes, but I have to protect you."

Jeffrey could, on occasion, take deadly aim, knowing the bull's-eye was big: "Maybe we're here because you haven't been able to pull it off."

Rachel looked directly at Cantwell, half expecting the big man to explode. Instead he glared. For a minute, nobody said anything. Cantwell finally spoke.

"Foolish thinking. Typical of people like you."

"Maybe. Maybe not." Rachel had little doubt that Jeffrey was right. "At any rate, we all want to find the same person. On that we can agree."

"Oh, we can agree on one thing more too. You're right, we all do want to find the same person. But the next part is that we're going to do it my way."

Jeffrey let out a little snort of contempt. Rachel tried to look chastened. If Cantwell thought he had at least one semiwilling collaborator, things might go better.

"What would you like us to do tomorrow?"

"More art galleries. What I've been trying to find is his gallery connection over here. We know about his gallery in the East."

"You mean he really has an art gallery?"

"Oh yes. About art, he's legitimate. Even has the credentials. But he uses it, just like he uses everything else."

"Well don't we all." Rachel smiled.

"I need a hot bath. My legs are killing me from riding that goddamned bicycle."

"Well, it was worth your while," Cantwell said. He was trying to make a peace, however fragile. "You did find where the forgeries are made. I expect your Mr. Steiner will float to one side of the Spree or the other by tomorrow morning."

"Not with those cans tied on him. Steiner is right at the bottom."

"Oh, they'll find him. Maybe not tomorrow, but soon."

"How?" Rachel asked.

"The river is just at the other side of the wall in that part of the city. It's full of devices and nets to keep people from getting across. They'll find him, but they won't care much."

□□□27 ∎

THE NEXT morning, not bright and not early, Jeffrey and Rachel went into the Steigenberger's *gemütlich* restaurant for breakfast before starting out to the art galleries. Rachel walked briskly past the ersatz brewery with its happy burghers painted on the wall. Jeffrey, legs sore from his bicycle ride, limped along behind her, but close enough to hear her exclaim. When he turned his gaze in the same direction as hers, he too saw Eddie Alvarez, severely jet-lagged, sitting at a table drinking coffee.

"I needed a vacation," Eddie told them, "and I kept thinking of the two of you here. Also, I've never been to Berlin. I've always wanted to see the Pergamon Museum . . . and the Altar."

"Good," Jeffrey said, smiling. "You can go into East Berlin with us tomorrow and we'll all see it."

"Is that really it?" Rachel asked. She had begun to suspect everybody of having unspecified motives and she wasn't about to exclude Detective Alvarez.

"Rachel, I ask you, what can an LAPD detective do in Berlin?"

"I don't really know."

"Well, I'll tell you. I haven't had any time off for three years. No great desire, really. But when I thought about it, I really did want to go somewhere . . . somewhere far away. And I love Europe, as people in my line of work usually do."

"Police?"

"No, art historians. I studied a summer in Italy, another in England. I've never done anything remotely spur-of-the-moment in my life. So I thought just this once . . . and with the two of you here there wouldn't be any reason to do it all alone. And I'm curious. So I called the IFAR people—I'm their West Coast representative, if you remember—and they thought it would be a good idea. They're not paying for it, but I think they will if we dig up something."

"Then let's go have an early lunch. Not here. There's a restaurant we're supposed to go to." Rachel had enough energy for all of them.

"Give me fifteen minutes to shower and wake up."

"You've got it," Jeffrey smiled.

They went, as Cantwell had suggested, to the Paris Bar. The hangout for artists and art dealers was packed even though it was not yet officially lunchtime. They had to lean forward to hear one another. The restaurant was old, with black-and-white tiled floors, maroon leather upholstery on the chairs and banquettes, and a series of forlorn plants in the windows forming a green buffer against the grim weather outside. As soon as they entered, an art dealer Rachel had met earlier came up to them, reintroduced himself, and asked if she had found any art to buy. He himself had more to show her. She took his card and thanked him, as Jeffrey stood silently by and Eddie watched.

"You've been looking around a bit."

"Quite a bit."

They told him everything: their tours of the galleries, their meetings with Cantwell, their invisible shadows, their day in East Berlin, the contact with Steiner. Jeffrey gave the details of his evening in East Berlin. Eddie listened, then shook his head.

"The trouble with the Steiners of this world," he said at last, "is that they're usually a couple tacos short of a full combo plate."

Rachel laughed. Jeffrey, who had seen too much, could only smile.

"And no sign of Wolfgang Dieter," Jeffrey told him finally.

"I'm not surprised," Eddie said. "And I have news for you."

Jeffrey and Rachel, whose chairs were close together because of the crowd, leaned forward across the table. Jeffrey knocked over the sugar jar, landing it on its snout and causing it to produce a mound of sugar, carefully measured. Their waiter saw the accident and quickly set it right. They waited until he was gone to talk more.

"Three more fake Stellas have turned up. One in Washington, D.C., and two in Los Angeles."

"Where in L.A.?" Rachel interrupted.

"At Benedict's . . . in Venice."

"They represent Stella on the West Coast."

"I know. And there's more. Nothing for sure yet, but the police in Chicago, New York, and in D.C. are slowly getting it together. It turns out there were unsolved murders in each city at approximately the time they suspect the art went into the galleries. All were supposedly drug-related, but all the dead men turn out to have burglary experience. Except that guy in San Francisco. The one who walked off with the Giacomettis. . . . That may have been a crucial error—at least it was enough to get the police looking."

"Jesus," Jeffrey muttered.

"So," Rachel thought aloud, "in each instance it's likely somebody—Dieter probably—hired someone to do the switch, then killed them after they had delivered the originals."

"Right. And there's more. A week ago today, eight Stellas—six from the *Had Gadya* series and two from the *River of Ponds* series—were shipped from New York to West Berlin. The documents don't show the exact names or the print numbers, but the coincidence is far too strong to ignore. Especially since no dealer in New York or Los Angeles who has Stellas for sale shipped any to Europe."

"Who from . . . and who to?" Jeffrey asked.

"From a professional freight forwarder in New York. The Treasury Department sent a customs officer to look at the forms. The sender, of course, turned out to be nonexistent. He paid in ¢ash, so no great effort was made to document who he was."

"Is that how it's usually done?" Jeffrey thought—despite his own experience—that the government might be more thorough.

"No, cash isn't used often, but it is used often enough so that nobody was suspicious. The point, really, for getting the sender's name and address correct is if there's any financial liability later. A lot of shippers have accounts with freight forwarders, so they keep better records of them. This one didn't. Cash on the line, and only the minimum of questions asked."

"And on this end?" Rachel expected more of the same, and that's what she got.

"A Berlin address. A warehouse not far from the Berlin Wall. The prints were delivered, the delivery was accepted, and all seemed to be in order."

"Except?"

"Except that when we contacted Berlin, the warehouse turned out to be abandoned, unused for five years.
Unused, that is, until they found the owner. He reported
renting it for two weeks and that he was paid in full, in
advance, and that when he went around to check on his
new tenants, they had been there and gone already—in
less than a day."

"What day?" Jeffrey leaned farther forward, and
Rachel grabbed the sugar jar before he spilled again.

Eddie looked at them evenly, ready to measure their
reactions. "The day before yesterday."

"So they're here . . . and so is Dieter."

"In all probability. Or at least not far from here."

"So you didn't come for vacation after all," Rachel
accused him.

"Oh, but I did. I came for vacation, and I came with
information. I also came with an idea. I wanted somehow
to combine police work with art history, and this is one
hell of a perfect project. I'm here as a doctoral candidate,
nothing more."

"But you're willing to help." Rachel made it less a
question and more statement of fact.

"Of course. Unofficially."

"That makes three of us." Jeffrey smiled.

"Three? Us?" Eddie's jet lag was getting the better of
him.

"We three . . . unofficial all."

"Doesn't that sort of piss off the professionals?"

"Cantwell's already thoroughly pissed off," Jeffrey
said. "There's something to this, I don't know what.
Somehow it has to do with Cantwell, but I'm not sure
how. He wants Dieter . . . and Dieter only. And he
doesn't give a damn about the art forgeries or anything
else."

"It figures," Eddie told them. He sat for a moment

thinking. "You've gotten yourself into something political. Cantwell and the CIA want Dieter. You want to stop the forgeries and find Henry's murderer. That is probably Dieter. I strongly suspect that the one has nothing to do with the other, that there is no great political motive behind these forgeries. It smells of sheer avarice to me, a big load of double-dealing that has nothing to do with politics."

"I suggest we eat," Rachel interrupted. Jeffrey smiled at her. Whenever Rachel's nerves got the best of her, her first instinct was to eat.

"And then, for me, some sleep." Eddie had no intention of joining in the visits to the art galleries.

"Here's to Henry," Rachel said quietly, raising her wineglass. "And to answers for Henry."

They drank quietly.

□□□ 28 ■

THEY CROSSED the next morning at Checkpoint Charlie, with Jeffrey and Rachel leading the way and Eddie several crossers behind them. They went without informing Cantwell. As they walked into no-man's-land at the border, Rachel turned and saw two men standing just outside the museum, watching them. She assumed they were their watchers and that their next move would be to call Cantwell. The three of them had discussed making their intentions known, but had decided against it. Cantwell might have had them stopped, and at any rate he'd find out soon enough they'd crossed.

They were going into East Berlin strictly as tourists. And that's what they were, armed with travel books, street maps, and a detailed guide to the Pergamon Museum. Jeffrey had his Nikon in his coat pocket, and before they crossed he slung it over his shoulder.

They headed up Friedrichstrasse, then on to Marx-Engels-Platz. The gray cloud cover had given way to a bright blue sky, and it seemed to Jeffrey and Rachel to be even colder than it had been earlier in the week. Eddie, unaccustomed to the weather, set the pace. They paused only on the bridge over the Kupfergraben River—the museum's entrance—to examine the war-torn facade.

"They began building it in 1903 and completed it in 1929, with time out for World War One," Eddie told them, the steam from his breath making brief clouds in the air. "And then it was practically ruined at the end of World War Two. Almost half the collection was destroyed."

"But not the really good stuff," Jeffrey countered.

"No, most of it survived."

They paid their entrance fee with the East German marks they had bought at Checkpoint Charlie, checked their coats, and Rachel and Eddie settled in for a long visit. Jeffrey, as he always did when starting through a museum, was seized by an urge to sit down for a while. Rachel knew this, and hid her amusement at Jeffrey's look of triumph when Eddie suddenly sat down and opened his book to read.

"I always do this," he explained, making himself comfortable. "Gives my feet a few minutes to recover . . . and lets me get my mind ready."

"I do too," Jeffrey said.

"More for your feet than your mind," Rachel commented, standing before them. Finally, she too sat down, and Eddie read aloud from his book on the museum.

"The Pergamon Altar is one of the wonders of the ancient world. The altar itself, dedicated to Zeus and Athena—tutelary goddess of the city of Pergamon in Asia Minor—dates from about 180 to 160 B.C., and was brought to Berlin in 1902. Look at this," he said, handing the book to Jeffrey. "Can you imagine what it must have been like to dig this thing up in 1902 and transport it stone by stone to Berlin?" He showed them an old photo of the dig site.

"Let's go see the real thing," Rachel said, no longer able to handle her impatience. "Eddie, if you sit there and read any longer you're going to give Jeffrey even worse habits than he already has."

They walked through two large rooms of antiquities and then turned left up a short ramp through a doorway and entered a huge sky-lighted room. There before them, occupying the entire length of the room, was the Altar— a marble monolith that struck Jeffrey as less like an altar and more like one of the buildings lining the boulevards of Paris. Except that every bit of it was intricately carved with the totems of ancient Asia—only its rows of pillars seemed, on closer look, to be familiar. Jeffrey looked at the expanse of steps leading to the Altar, then peered more closely.

"Those steps are very small. The whole scale of the thing is small, almost as if it's a model, not the real thing."

"People were a lot smaller then," Eddie commented, not looking at him but concentrating on one of the murals anchored to the wall opposite the Altar.

They remained there for about fifteen minutes, then walked into the next room, which contained the gate to the Roman market in Miletus, a monumental piece of early Greek architecture that was shrouded in scaffolding and plastic.

"Looks like this was hit by a bomb," Eddie remarked.

"Sort of what the whole place must have looked like at one time," Jeffrey added.

"It's being restored," Rachel said, pulling a loose piece of paper from Eddie's book, "by"—and she read— "funds collected from the cement workers of the German Democratic Republic."

"Or else," Eddie added.

The museum had few visitors—Rachel assumed be-

cause it was a weekday morning and a cold one at that—
so there were no crowds to contend with, no restless
groups of children being herded through for a mandatory
dose of culture, and very few people walking,
guidebooks in hand, contemplating room after room of
wonders, any one of which would have been the foundation for an entire museum in the United States.

From the market gate they trod their way across
wooden scaffolding into the long narrow room containing the Ishtar gate and the processional leading up to
it, which lined the long walls of the room. The gate itself
had once been part of the facade for the throne room in
ancient Babylon. The Pergamon Altar had been all white
marble, almost an illusion. The Babylonians, on the other
hand, loved color. The gate and the walls leading up to it
were a riot of bright tiles, richly ornamented. In the center of the room, in an enclosed glass case, was a model of
Babylon. They each examined the model, then looked at
the walls and gate to find exactly where they were in ancient Babylon. Rachel was intrigued by the color, Eddie
by the architecture, and Jeffrey was thinking that Cecil B.
De Mille's vulgar epics must have been closer to the truth
than anyone had believed. Each was alone with his fan-
tasies, lost in another millennium, adrift in one of the
world's greatest and most inaccessible museums.

"A designer friend told me once that much of the in-
spiration for American Art Deco design came from this
room."

They all turned to see who was speaking. Eddie and
Jeffrey knew by instinct, Rachel the second she saw him.
All three froze.

"Can you imagine what your Barbra Streisand would
want to do with this room? She has one of the great Art
Deco collections in America. I once sold several pieces to
her through a friend."

"Did your friend live to tell about the experience?" Jeffrey said evenly.

"Of course." Wolfgang Dieter smiled politely at them. "What would be the purpose?" He was exactly as she remembered him, his tailoring perfect, his manners impeccable. "I don't believe we've met," he said, removing a glove and extending his hand to Eddie. "I'm Wolfgang Dieter. Miss Sabin knows me as Karl Diedrich."

"Edward Alvarez."

"Ah, of the Los Angeles Police Department. What brings you to Berlin?"

"Curiosity."

"I think that is a large part of the reason for Mr. Dean and Miss Sabin's visit too. That, and their desire to find an answer to what happened to their friend Mr. Thurmond."

"You, of course, know all about it—intimately," Rachel shot back at him.

"I know, yes. Intimately, no."

"Are you an agent for the East German government?" Rachel asked.

"Yes," he said, smiling.

There was nowhere they could go, no possible escape. They all wished now that they had asked for Cantwell's protection before they crossed the border. Even that might have been of little good, but at least it was something.

"I can imagine how you feel just now. However, you are safe; nothing will happen to you. I was going to come into the West later today and find you, but this is so much safer for me right now. And I had made the assumption that as people of some culture you would want to come here."

"How did you know?" Rachel asked. Her fear, her panic, made her voice seem constrained and tight.

"I was telephoned as soon as you came through the border. Our guards may not be what you Americans call good public-relations men, but they are all very efficient. You were followed here. I left instructions you were to be detained if I could not reach you in time. Fortunately, that was not necessary. There is a café near here, with good coffee and even better food. I would be honored to have you as my guests."

They had no choice, and so they collected their coats and silently bundled up while Dieter stood patiently waiting for them. He politely gestured them through the revolving doors, and once outside, he stopped and spoke quietly to them.

"I promise you, within an hour, I will take you back to what you call Checkpoint Charlie and I will show you safely across."

"We obviously have no choice," Eddie muttered.

"Precisely," Dieter said. "The café is just a few blocks to your left. We will be undisturbed there."

☐☐☐ 29 ■

THE CAFÉ, with its tiled floors, zinc bar, and intricately carved ceiling was prewar, one of the few Berlin buildings to escape the deadly attack that came from both east and west. Dieter showed them to a corner table near a window, gestured them to chairs, and—after politely consulting with them—ordered espresso for all. He frowned in mock chagrin when his guests, as he insisted on calling them, refused his offer of pastries.

"Perhaps another time," he said finally.

"When hell freezes over," Jeffrey said quietly but emphatically.

"I don't know about hell, but I will tell you Berlin is about to freeze over."

"Why did you kill those people?" Rachel asked.

"You mean Henry Thurmond, don't you, Miss Sabin?"

"Henry and the others."

"You get right to the point, I see. The hardest thing I have to do in this meeting is to convince you I did not kill any of them. Mr. Thurmond included."

There was no reply.

"Perhaps I should start from the beginning. I did not misrepresent myself to you, Miss Sabin. I indeed own a gallery in Berlin . . . East Berlin. It is my avocation. I have two advanced degrees in art history, one of them from the Courtauld in London."

"You studied under Anthony Blunt?" Jeffrey was intrigued.

" 'Under' is an unfortunate word in this instance. He was my professor, yes."

"And your contact?"

"No. I was his contact. But that is another story. I grew up in a family which appreciated fine art, and one which collected it. At the end of the war, we were like other Berliners—we had nothing. My father was dead and, so that we could eat, my mother became a *Trümmerfrau,* a woman of the ruins, who eked out survival by collecting rubble. She was dead within two years. I had no family left, but I did have—in three especially built rooms at the bottom of an old barn not very far from here—my family's art collection. It formed the nucleus of my business."

"You were allowed to keep it?" Eddie was puzzled.

"Of course. By the time they discovered I had such a collection, I was a person of some responsibility. It was thought fitting—particularly for my official work—that I be allowed to keep it, and to open a business."

An unsmiling waiter wearing a stained white apron placed their coffee before them. Dieter stopped talking until he had gone.

"My art was, as you Westerners might say it, my cover. It enabled me to travel to places and move among people I might never have otherwise met. I am also something of a problem to the people on the other side of the wall"—his head moved in the general direction of the wall itself—"because I do in fact do business with a number of art dealers in Berlin. They know, or at least suspect, my other job but it does not matter. They have become friends and it is always handled very discreetly. So you see, I have experience and access."

"Why forge art, then?" Jeffrey asked.

"I don't. The first forged prints, Stellas not dissimilar to those which have appeared in the United States, turned up in Berlin. West Berlin. I was alerted. I put some of my people on it, but unofficially, since it appeared to have no bearing on my official work. To my horror I discovered the prints themselves are probably made here in the East. I do not know for sure how they are transported from East to West, but it will be only a matter of time until I have the answer to that. Nor do I know where the printing is done."

Jeffrey looked quickly at Eddie and Rachel. If Dieter noticed, he pretended not to. Their agreement was silent: Now was not the time to tell. Dieter continued.

"What I have also learned is that the operation is run from West Berlin. I have made absolutely no progress at finding out where; I have only a small amount of information. That's where you come in."

"Oh?" Rachel leaned back in her chair, her coffee untouched.

"I would guess, knowing how he operates, that your Mr. Cantwell has not exactly been forthright about why you are in Berlin."

"We're here to look for you." Jeffrey looked directly at him. "And I don't imagine you're a paragon of candor either."

"I leave it to the three of you to decide about that, all in good time. But if you are here to find me, why? To find out who is killing off people and stealing art in your country?"

"Yes," Rachel said. "Exactly."

"Not so. You are here to lure me into the West so that I can be captured. I am what you Americans call a big fish in this little pond here. They want to catch me."

"Why?" Eddie thought he knew the answer, but he wanted to hear it from Dieter.

"Because, Mr. Alvarez, I trouble them. I know too much, much more than they think I do. And I cause them a lot of problems. Ask your Mr. Cantwell about Fölker Köberling."

"Fölker Köberling?" Jeffrey asked. It wasn't so much a question as an attempt to commit the name to memory.

"Fölker Köberling came to Mr. Cantwell four years ago with important information, information which proved to be absolutely correct. He became trusted by Mr. Cantwell . . ."

"And he was one of yours." Eddie finished the sentence for him.

"Oh yes, he was one of ours. Mr. Cantwell literally turned his people inside out when he discovered what was going on. Fölker Köberling, meanwhile, had come back to the East."

Jeffrey nodded. He'd figured it was something like this.

"And that isn't all. There are others. That is how it works here in Berlin. Your Mr. Cantwell wants me, because I know the answers. I have been lucky at my work. My opponent has not."

Not one of Dieter's audience of three believed luck had anything to do with it. Cantwell had been outclassed and outmaneuvered, and he was angry. Dieter confirmed it:

"Fölker Köberling made his escape a month ago. Since then, my opponent has been, as you Americans say, on the warpath. He has made it virtually impossible for me to cross into the West.

"So, along you come. Two people in Los Angeles who are in the art and rare-book business. I visit your gallery and sell you a Stella. You identify me somehow. So off you go to Berlin, with your government's blessing, to look for me. But you do not really know the reason you are being allowed to look for me."

"It was a fake Stella and Henry died because of it," Rachel said.

"I know, and for that I am deeply sorry. I did not expect you to give the Stella to Mr. Thurmond that night at your house."

"You knew about our dinner?" Rachel was now astonished.

"Only that you had a guest for dinner, and I knew who that guest was. Our stakeout of your house ended before Mr. Thurmond left. . . .with the Stella. That was my big mistake."

"But why?" Rachel was trying to understand.

"I was not alone. Two of my colleagues were with me, though they were traveling separately—which is how we do those things. We had a lead, from here, who was carrying the forged art and who was making the arrangements. We followed him from New York to Chicago to New Orleans to San Francisco. We nearly caught him in Los Angeles. Instead, you gave the Stella print to Mr. Thurmond, so it was not in your house when he came to look for the original."

"Now I really am confused," Jeffrey said.

"I understand that. Give me a few more minutes. The man made more than one mistake in San Francisco. His exchange was discovered because he chose the wrong person to make the switch. And the other Stella he was to substitute was purchased the day before he made the switch."

"Purchased by you?"

"Yes. It was a relatively easy guess. One print from

the *River of Ponds* series was exchanged in New Orleans, so I knew there had to be another forgery—they are far too complicated to produce to make only one. We are carefully trained to place ourselves in the minds of the people we seek. That's what I did. It really wasn't all that difficult. I began calling dealers around the country, and when I finally found another *River of Ponds* print for sale it was in San Francisco. I bought it before Mueller could get to it."

"Mueller?" All three of them spoke at the same time.

"Bear with me; I will explain. When I made the purchase I pretended I was you, Mr. Dean, and that I was making the purchase for Miss Sabin's gallery."

"What the hell did you do that for?"

"As I said, I was trying to think like Mueller. I presumed—a very safe presumption—that he had one more print from the *Had Gadya* series to exchange. And I found out the only one left was, or so I thought at the time, in your gallery."

"How did you find that out?" Jeffrey wasn't sure whether to be impressed or simply astounded.

"You'd be surprised how easy it is. Each print, each painting by Frank Stella is recorded by his dealer in New York. Every time an associated dealer sells something, a call is made to New York and the name and address of the purchaser is recorded. Quite a few major artists do this now, so that a record can be kept of their work for museum shows and things like that.

"But you, it turns out, are not quite like other gallery owners," Dieter continued, smiling at Miss Sabin. "You did not put the *Had Gadya* print up for sale, did not store it in your gallery. Instead, you took it home and the two of you, one rainy night, hung it on the wall of your living room."

"You were watching, I gather." Rachel said coldly.

"Not me, someone else. But it was me who sold the other print to you, and I daresay you got quite a bargain. I paid three thousand dollars more for it than I sold it to you for. That was the trap, and we were waiting for him."

"What happened?"

"You took the smaller print home and so when he entered your gallery he could not find it. Nor did he find it at your home."

"That explains the two robberies where nothing was missing."

"Precisely."

"How did he find it?"

"More coffee? And maybe now some pastries? Or sandwiches?" He waved for the waiter, and this time Eddie, Rachel, and Jeffrey all ordered something, their suspicion lessened by facts finally fitting together.

"Go on," Eddie said.

"Very well then. Miss Sabin, at this point I must make a few assumptions, all based on the fact that I knew Mueller found Henry Thurmond. Perhaps he was among the people at your show, though he was not there while I was. Or he did some asking around and learned who Thurmond was. I am not sure."

"I think I can help there." Rachel, who had been fairly reticent and had been listening closely, finally spoke up. She saw the others all turn their eyes on her. "I received a telephone call from Henry, along with one or two other calls, during a meeting with a museum support group. I was alone in the gallery so I left my phone machine on. I heard it ring, and I made a mental note to check the machine later. After my visitors departed, I left the gallery open and ran across the patio to get myself an iced tea. I was very hot."

"And?" Dieter was intrigued.

"When I got back to the gallery I went to collect the messages. I just remembered now. The call counter did not show the number of messages, even though I had heard them being left. I played back the messages and they were all there, including one from Henry saying he had an idea for the Stella, and asking me to call him. He left his new direct-dial office telephone number. I wrote it down. Then I had to lock up—it was so hot I'd even left the back door open; the air conditioning wasn't working well. My guess, if what you're saying is true, is that this man came into the gallery and got the messages. He could have been standing at the door waiting when they came in. Or he played them back when I left for iced tea. In any case, I would not have seen him." She shuddered.

Dieter nodded in satisfaction. "A shot in the dark by Mueller, but one that hit its target. It could very well be."

"So, the switch was made. But with a difference." Jeffrey was already there. "This Mueller had to get it, and to get it he had to murder the owner this time."

"Right. He had already been there. We almost caught up with him as he was making the switch on the big Stellas in Los Angeles. He exchanged three in a gallery in Venice, and then set out to find the *River of Ponds*. I'm assuming he simply gave up on the big Stella in your living room because there was no way he could really switch it, given its heavy frame."

"It took at least two people just to lift it," Rachel agreed.

"So he went after the smaller print, the one he assumed Henry had. Except that Henry didn't have it, it was at the museum to be reframed."

"Is that reason to kill Henry?" Rachel asked.

"For Mueller, yes. Somehow, I don't know how,

Mueller established, under one pretense or another, some contact with Mr. Thurmond. That's why he had to die. Mueller found out where the print was, then murdered. The obvious reason is that Henry could identify him. Maybe not right then when nobody knew what was going on, but eventually. The other reason is that Mueller murders. He does not care who."

Eddie, whose stoic countenance seldom betrayed emotion, suddenly sat straight up in his chair. "Who is Mueller?"

The coffee and sandwiches were served. By this time the waiter had deduced his customers were not exactly ordinary. The service improved considerably, with the server sporting a clean apron. Dieter noticed the change and so did Rachel. Jeffrey and Eddie were gazing out the window, thinking.

"Henrik Mueller is a terrorist. I knew it was him by the time I got to New Orleans, because he always visited the galleries first, to make sure the prints he wanted were there, so by that time I had three different gallery owners identifying him, and I had time to get back to my people to make certain. Mueller is the son of a well-to-do West German businessman. He is a psychopath, as most terrorists are. I am not proud of the fact that in Moscow there are people who seek out men and women like Mueller, but there are. He was sent to Patrice Lumumba University, trained extensively, and put to work. Unlike others of his sort, Mueller is spoiled and likes to live well. So when he is not going about planting bombs and blowing up airplanes with his colleagues, he makes a living on the side."

Dieter stopped, took a bite of his sandwich, and looked at the others. "Mueller is your murderer. And he is here in Berlin. In the West, because he is not permitted to operate on his own in the East."

"And you want to find him," Jeffrey finished the thought.

"Yes. And the people doing the forgeries on this side, and doing the business on yours. And I want to stop them."

"How?"

"Each night, a truck loaded with fresh fruit crosses from the West into the East. My colleagues, or at least those high enough who have lived outside in the West, have developed a taste for certain luxuries not available to us. Fresh fruit is one, so the government has arranged for a shipment each night. There are three trucks involved, one busy collecting the fruit while a second, already loaded, makes the trip across. The third is used when the others break down. I am quite certain that at least one of the trucks does not return empty. The forged prints are somewhere on it. I will know for sure tonight. Tomorrow, I will begin tracing them. I would like you, meanwhile, to do some detective work for me."

"Such as?" Jeffrey's common sense told him to refuse, but he had a stronger instinct to say yes.

"I will find out where the truck stops here, where the art is loaded. Then you will follow it when it goes back across the border. And then follow whoever takes the forgeries off. It will happen tonight."

"How do you know?"

"Mueller bought a plane ticket to New York yesterday. The plane leaves tomorrow afternoon. He's back in business."

"How do you know so much about what's going on in West Berlin?" Eddie was testing, but only slightly.

"For one thing I am what they call a *Grenzgänger,* a border crosser. I go across often, or at least I did until Mr. Cantwell and his people intensified their search for me. Berlin, Mr. Alvarez, has been said to be an

agentensumpf, a spy swamp. That is exactly so. Some of
the best of them work for me. That's how I found out
about Mueller's plane ticket."

Dieter took a small leather-bound notebook out of his
coat, and a pen. "Here is a telephone number where you
can reach me. There is no problem calling across the wall
on this line, only please do not let Cantwell have it until
we have finished all of this. And here"—he withdrew a
photograph from his coat—"is Mueller. Stay away from
him."

The photograph was of a tall blond man with intense
eyes, sunken cheekbones, and a receding hairline. He appeared nondescript—all the better, Eddie thought, for a
terrorist.

Jeffrey turned pale. He had seen Mueller before, the
night he murdered Steiner.

"Does he know of us?" Rachel had noticed Jeffrey's
reaction, but did not understand it.

"Probably. I would assume yes, so do not even let
him see you. You, Mr. Alvarez, I doubt he knows. But if
you see him, stay away, all of you."

There was a brief silence, and then Dieter ended the
meeting. "I hope you believe what I have told you. It is
the truth."

"Glasnost?" Eddie asked.

Dieter smiled. "I don't know about glasnost. It is a
good idea in theory, but one wonders about the practice
of it. We are, after all, enemies for many years. Such
things do not end on a word, or even with time. Now.
You are to proceed directly to the border crossing. It will
be to your right as you leave this café. Once you see the
Pergamon, you'll know your way back. There will be no
trouble. You are being watched, and the Vopos expect
you at the border. I wish you the best of luck. If I have
not heard from one of you by midnight tonight, I will
call you."

□□□ **30** ■

WHILE THEY were still in no-man's-land, but nevertheless across the border, Jeffrey, who could barely contain himself, spoke.

"That picture. The photograph of Mueller?" Eddie and Rachel nodded. "That's the man who killed Steiner."

"Good God. Maybe Dieter is right." Rachel stopped and stood still. Jeffrey reached back to pull her along.

They had made their plans by the time they crossed back through Checkpoint Charlie. The Vopos had been expecting them and the crossing took less than ten minutes. Dieter was as good as his word. As they had agreed, Eddie slipped behind, so he would not be noticed by Cantwell's watchers. They figured Eddie's presence had not yet been discovered and, for now, they needed whatever advantage they had.

Rachel and Jeffrey spotted their tails the minute they entered the final part of the crossing zone. They were waiting, binoculars in hand, inside the American portion of the three-powers building. One of them gave a little

wave of recognition while the other reached for a telephone.

"We've been worried about you," one said as he fell
into step with them. The other put down the telephone
and followed. "Theo will meet us back at your hotel."

"We decided to spend the day at the Pergamon,"
Rachel said, quietly offering an answer where no question
was asked. Nothing more was said on the short ride back
to the Steigenberger. They had settled back into padded
chairs in the lounge and ordered tea when Cantwell, coat-
tails flying, hurried into the room. Like many overweight
people, he was remarkably light on his feet and graceful.

"What the hell did you do that for?" He sat down
without greeting them.

"We decided to spend the day at the Pergamon,"
Jeffrey quickly answered, pulling his travel books and
museum guide from his coat pocket.

"And you saw Dieter."

Their pause gave them away. They hadn't expected
the question. At least not quite yet, and not as a statement.

"Why didn't you let us know?"

"How could we," Rachel said as politely as she could.
"We didn't expect to see him. He just showed up while
we were in the Pergamon. At the gate to Babylon."

"Just showed up? That can't be."

"He said he had us followed, then came to see us."

"Oh, God." Cantwell slumped in his chair, put his
hands to the side of his head as though he were dealing
with two recalcitrant teenagers. "What did he tell you?"

"That you were looking for him, wanted to trap him
in the West," Jeffrey said, "and that the pressure was on."

"Give me details."

Jeffrey told the story, omitting, as they'd all agreed,
Dieter's request that they help him end the forgeries. As

Eddie suggested—reasoning the truth was easier for all of them to keep their stories together—Jeffrey spared no detail, right down to Mueller and back to the night in East Berlin when he killed Steiner.

"Christ. You really messed it up. I told you, I wanted you to lure him over here. You were not supposed to go back across."

Rachel looked up and saw Eddie walk into the room, open a newspaper, and sit down at a table nearby.

"We only went to see the Pergamon," Rachel said, wondering if it was really true.

"Well, good for you. You saw it."

"I should think you'd be relieved. Dieter is not your murderer according to him, and I think he's right. What about Mueller?"

"We'll go after him just in case. But I want Dieter." Cantwell, clearly frustrated and angry, slapped a hand on his leg.

"Why?"

"I say he's involved in this, every bit of it, right down to collecting the loot."

"Have you evidence?"

"Never mind that. You're here to help us, and what you did today was no help at all. No goddamn help at all."

"Was Fölker Köberling any help?" Jeffrey's retort was pointed, and instead of exploding, Cantwell imploded. His face reddened, his hands gripping the arm of the chair.

"So the bastard brags too." That was all he had to say. It was enough.

"We're here to find the people who murdered Henry Thurmond," Jeffrey said evenly, "and, if we can, help you break up this forgery business."

"Uhmmm." Cantwell's thoughts were, for the moment, elsewhere, in some elaborately constructed conundrum only people in his profession could understand.

"Isn't that so?" Rachel pressed him, sensing they were near the truth.

"Right." His scowl turned to a smile. "And we'll get him yet. Did he give you a telephone number or any other way of contacting him?"

"No," Rachel lied. "He told us he'd be in touch. Probably within the next two days."

"All right, then listen carefully. I want you to keep going to art galleries, make all the right moves. When he contacts you, no matter when or where, you make sure we know about it immediately. And one more thing, I want you to make sure to spread the word among gallery owners that Dieter's involved in a forgery ring."

They nodded in apparent comprehension.

"Do you think he'll come over here looking for us?" Jeffrey finally asked.

"I sure as hell hope so. If not, we'll come up with another plan. The deal"—to emphasize his point he leaned across the small table and poked a defiant and chubby finger into it for emphasis—"is to get Dieter and put him out of commission. For good."

Jeffrey turned to Rachel, watched her stare into her cup of tea. They knew now.

"We will contact you immediately when we hear from him," Jeffrey lied. Rachel quickly looked up, but Cantwell did not notice.

As soon as Cantwell—pleading an appointment at the consulate—departed, Rachel picked up her coat and purse and headed for their room. On the way, she stopped at Eddie's table. Jeffrey followed her and, a few minutes later, Eddie knocked at the door to their room.

"You know what I think?" he said, even before he sat down on the edge of their bed.

"That Dieter is telling the truth," Jeffrey responded immediately.

"Right. He may not be on our side technically, but he's with us philosophically. If you get what I'm driving at."

"Oh, we get it," Rachel said. "It's Mueller."

"Mueller and the people he works for here in the West. If we're lucky, we'll find out who that is tonight."

"What if we also find out Dieter is part of it in some way?" Rachel wondered aloud.

"Yes, let's keep that very much in mind," Eddie said. "I doubt it, but remember where we are. Nothing is what it seems in this place."

"All right. We're committed. I'm going to call Dieter and tell him where the printing is done and what I saw there, that it was Mueller."

Eddie agreed after a moment's deliberation. Rachel, less trusting, took longer.

"It's not a matter of trust," Jeffrey argued. "I trust Dieter only a little bit more than Cantwell, and him I don't trust at all. What it is is sharing what we know, and protecting ourselves a bit in the process."

"That, and Dieter will know that Mueller is aware of you both and knows your names. That can help us," Eddie added.

"All right," she agreed. "But I wish I knew what happened to Henry. It doesn't make sense. I know, and Dieter confirms it, that Henry took an original Stella home with him that night. At some point the switch was made, but when? How did Mueller do it?"

They fell silent, each of them alone with their private suppositions. Jeffrey and Rachel mentally retraced their last night with Henry, dealing, as was their nature, with images. Eddie remembered too, but his recollections were practical. He was, after all, a cop. He ran down the list of people he had questioned about Henry. It wasn't a long list, and he was only halfway through it when he looked up.

"Shit. I think I've got it. I'll have to make a call to Los Angeles, but I think I know what happened. I'll explain it later tonight. If I'm right."

"I hope you are," Rachel told him. "That's what we're all here for."

Half an hour later, Eddie was in the hotel dining room eating dinner, still fighting his jet lag, and Rachel and Jeffrey were back at the Paris Bar, playing, as Jeffrey put it, "Caesar's wife," making sure they were seen to be above suspicion.

At 11:30, they met again in the hotel room.

"Did you get through to Los Angeles?" Rachel asked as Eddie walked into the room.

"Yes. But it was too early in the morning. I'm going to call again later."

They settled back to wait. Jeffrey was poring over guide maps, Rachel was looking out their hotel-room window, and Eddie was sitting by the telephone. They waited. Dieter's call came exactly at midnight. Eddie answered it.

"The truck dropped off the fruit, then was driven to a factory down by the Spree. Right where you said it was, Jeffrey. Dieter says the flatbed has a false floor, and cardboard tubes were placed in it. He's certain it's the prints. He says it will come back across the border around"—Eddie looked at his watch—"two A.M. I have the license number."

As they had agreed earlier in the evening, Eddie had left immediately after his dinner and rented a car. It was parked directly in front of the hotel.

"Why doesn't he do it himself?" Rachel asked. "He must have people over here who could do this for him."

"I think Dieter wants us involved. He's making a point. And, frankly, I'm willing," Jeffrey answered her.

"Me too," Eddie added.

Rachel nodded her agreement. "Bundle up—it's going to be cold."

"That fits. After all, we're involved in the cold war now," Jeffrey remarked. His attempt at humor was lost on Rachel and Eddie.

Jeffrey and Rachel headed for the hotel lounge and the back way past the samovar shop. Eddie went directly out the front door, and drove around to the side street to meet them. It was a new Volvo two-door, so Rachel climbed into the backseat. Eddie made several wrong turns, and it required all three of them to navigate their way back to Checkpoint Charlie. They parked at the empty taxi stand beside the museum Jeffrey and Rachel had visited two days before. Jeffrey left and walked around the corner, where he could see anyone crossing the border.

They waited. Rachel and Eddie could see Jeffrey in the shadow outside the street lights, huddled up against the door to a chemist's shop. It was almost an hour later when he started back to the car.

"There's a big Mercedes truck crossing now," he said as he scrambled into the seat and reached his hands out to the heater. He read off the license number.

"That's it," Eddie said. They heard the high whine of the truck's diesel engine before they saw it. It rounded the corner and headed directly for them. Rachel and Jeffrey ducked down in their seat. Eddie, jammed behind the steering wheel and unable to hide, cursed as the headlight beams flashed across his face.

"I thought they'd go the other way," Eddie commented as he put the car in gear and began his turn. They didn't have to go far. Traffic in this part of the all-night city was almost nonexistent, so they stayed a good distance back. The truck drove past the Springer Tower and continued on, traveling parallel to the wall. Then, without signaling, it pulled into an alley that was a dead end smack against the wall. The lights from the guard towers could not be seen as they drove past the alley. Eddie quickly turned away from the wall into a street leading back toward the city. Jeffrey jumped out and ran back, after motioning for Rachel and Eddie to stay in the car.

He was back, less than five minutes later, winded, his words forming dense little clouds of steam as he leaned in the window.

"There was a car waiting. The truck pulled in, the driver opened the floor, and ten tubes went into the car. Turn around quick."

Eddie, trained at tailing, quickly complied. Jeffrey ran back to the corner, stopped, and peered around it. He motioned them forward.

"There. About two blocks down. The black sedan. BMW." He stuck his hand into his mouth, pulled off his glove, then reached inside his jacket for pen and paper. He quickly wrote down the license number.

"He's going back into the center of the city," Eddie commented. "It'll be easier to follow him in traffic."

The BMW turned short of the center of the city, down one empty street and then another. Jeffrey could see the sweat forming on Eddie's forehead despite the cold. Finally, from a distance of two blocks, they saw the car turn into an alley and slow down. They moved forward more, pulled into a parking place, and turned off their lights. They watched as one man jumped out and unlocked a door that appeared to them to be the rear entrance to a store. The other loaded his arms with tubes and carried them inside. It took two trips to unload them all. The other man returned to the car and parked it, then they both went inside the building.

"Keithstrasse," Eddie said, rubbing the condensation from the driver's window and peering at the street sign.

"What?" Rachel asked, shivering in the cold.

"Keithstrasse. Very fashionable. Old valuable furniture," Jeffrey said, turning in her direction.

"How'd you know that?" Eddie asked.

"I read guidebooks."

"Drive around the front so we'll know for sure we have the right place," Jeffrey insisted. Eddie drove quickly around the block.

"Number forty-four," Jeffrey noted.

They left the car and stood bundled and shivering on the corner, out of sight of the building.

"Here's what we'll do. Rachel and I will walk down the street. If anyone sees us we'll pretend to be drunk. Jeffrey, you go around the block from the other direction. We'll meet right back here."

It was a short walk. Keithstrasse was a small street between two main boulevards, and it was door-to-door antique shops, all with elegant displays in their windows. There were apartments along the street as well, all above the stores or connected by short walkways to buildings off the street. Number 44 had a simple gold sign in its window reading ANTIQUARIAT. No lights were on in the store itself, but the apartment directly above it provided almost the only light falling onto the street.

"What now?" Rachel asked when they met back at the corner.

"I wait," Eddie told them. "There's a small café near the corner and it'll be open in a couple of hours. Until then I'm going to do some brisk walking. The two of you go back to the hotel and call Dieter. I'll call you at seven A.M."

"I've got a better idea. Eddie, you watch for an hour and a half, I'll take the next shift, and Jeffrey the next. By then we'll have contacted Dieter and we'll know what to do next."

"No." Eddie was accustomed to issuing orders in such circumstances. "No way. I'm staying. Jeffrey can stay. You go back to the hotel, call Dieter, and wait. Rachel, I don't think it will be safe for you here. You have no way of physically defending yourself if something happens. Jeffrey does, but not like I do. I wait. You go. I want to be around here when the place starts to wake up, and I'm better trained for dealing with things like this—I don't want either of you to encounter these people alone."

They agreed, Rachel reluctantly. Jeffrey decided to accompany Rachel back to the hotel, call Dieter, and then return to report on the conversation.

"You be here. Don't do anything without us," he cautioned.

"If I'm not here, you'll know where to find me," Eddie said, nodding his head in the direction of 44 Keith-strasse.

□□□ 31 ■

EDDIE STOOD back in a doorway, two stores away and across Keithstrasse from number 44. A vague hint of the daylight to come appeared in the cold, dark air. Almost a promise. The lights in the apartment still burned. No one had appeared on the street. He had been there nearly two hours before he heard footsteps approaching. Jeffrey walked past him.

"I'm in here."

"Jesus!" Jeffrey jumped, then smiled when he saw Eddie huddled in the corner, his arms folded under his topcoat, his gloved hands stuffed in his armpits for warmth. "I think I know why there are no street people in Berlin."

"Very tidy, these Germans. What did Dieter say?"

"Help is on the way. He's sending two men to help us watch."

"I've got a plan."

"Dieter said don't do anything until his men get here."

"Don't worry. I'm too cold to move. I meant later.
Like at ten A.M. when the antique shop opens."

Eddie explained his idea. Jeffrey listened, then nodded.

"It might just work," he said finally.

"Maybe we ought to alert Cantwell."

"No, don't. If this works, we'll get our answer. Our
way."

"Strange place, this city. What did Dieter call it, a spy
swamp?"

Jeffrey nodded, then shifted his position slightly.

"We all of us go through life surrounded by our fears,
our problems, our own state of mental health," Eddie
went on. "But all of that comes from inside us. Here, it's
as though that state exists both inside people and around
them. I feel outside of myself here, if that makes any
sense. Surrounded."

"You are surrounded."

"So is Berlin."

"That's just it."

"Do you ever miss journalism—the action?"

Jeffrey thought for a moment, and then answered. It
was the sort of question posed from one good friend to
another late at night after too much drinking.

"Yes. Yes, I do. When I became a book dealer I was
fed up, with journalism, with what was going on in the
world. My biggest problem was that I was an observer,
and I felt somehow without influence, that I couldn't
change what I was observing. And I finally felt I was
even observing my own life, having no impact on it at
all. I wanted out, and I got out. Now, several years have
passed and it seems to me there won't be many chances
to get back in for one last ride. Probably none at all. I just
don't know. I've been thinking about going back, maybe

to a newspaper, but I'm not certain. I used to crave action, now I just miss it. What about you?"

"You're in the action now." Eddie was smiling, Jeffrey could tell from his eyes, but he couldn't see his lips—the bottom of his face was wrapped in his wool scarf. "I feel like you do, only I'm at the opposite end of it. I was thinking a few minutes ago about how when this is all wrapped up, I'd like to get out and finish my doctorate. Then teach. But sure as hell, I'd miss being a cop. And I've only got seven years to go before I can retire."

"Where is it written that you aren't allowed to live in the real world, and then pull out for a while?"

"Everywhere," Eddie answered. He tried, without success, to slip his head farther into his topcoat. "How well did you know Henry Thurmond?"

"We've told you. Quite well. We also like . . . liked him very much."

Eddie paused, thought it over one more time, and decided to proceed. "There's one thing I didn't tell you about his death. He had had anal intercourse."

"With Mueller?"

"Probably. We won't be able to tell until we get Mueller's blood type. But the pubic hair on Henry's body is the right color for Mueller."

"Jesus."

"You didn't know about Henry?"

"We assumed, that's all. Rachel didn't care; neither did I. I don't believe in judging people by their sexual preference. We all play the cards we're dealt. Henry got a different hand than most people. What I don't like is having someone cut him up and discover such an intimate thing."

"I have a reason for telling you," Eddie persisted. "The coroner is certain the sex act took place following death."

Jeffrey closed his eyes, in pain—and out of respect—for his dead friend. "Mueller is homosexual. And a necrophiliac."

"And very goddamn dangerous. That's why I'm telling you."

Jeffrey nodded. "Just don't tell Rachel." He turned to see Eddie agree with a shake, almost a shiver. A car drove by, its sound muffled by the snow on the street. They could see two men in it.

"That must be them. Dieter said they'd meet us outside the café just around the corner. You go first, Eddie. I'll follow."

The two men were big and nontalkative—Jeffrey figured Dieter was calling in his heavies in case there was trouble. The café wasn't yet open, so they held a brief conversation, then one of Dieter's men went to take the car around so that it was close to the alleyway, while the other took up watch in Eddie's doorway. Eddie and Jeffrey walked three blocks before finding a cab, and returned immediately to the warmth of the Steigenberger's coffee shop.

"Do you have a gun with you?" Rachel asked when Eddie explained his plan. She was reluctant, and wanted to know the odds.

"No," Eddie answered matter-of-factly. "But I've got years of karate and defense training with me. And I'm good at games."

"It's no game, Eddie."

"It can be made to seem like it, if I play it right."

Rachel finally agreed, just as Eddie began to think of the difficulties in obtaining a consensus in a democracy, even in a democracy of three. That wouldn't happen if this were Los Angeles and he was in charge. At quarter of ten in the morning, Jeffrey, Rachel, and Eddie—all dressed as though for a day of business—left the Steigen-

berger and took a taxi to the café around the corner from
44 Keithstrasse.

The sun was up and the air felt warmer, but not by
much. Rachel and Jeffrey walked down one side of the
street, while Eddie went down the other. They saw Eddie stop and speak briefly to the man still standing in the
doorway. Then all three met at the opposite end of the
street.

Eddie looked at his watch. It was five minutes after
ten. The business day had begun, and they had all seen
shopkeepers unlocking their doors along the street. "OK,
here goes." He walked back down the street, opened the
door of number 44, and walked into the shop.

Rachel and Jeffrey went directly to the café, found a
table near the window, and sat down. They were too
nervous to eat, so they ordered only coffee. Jeffrey
looked around at the other customers, hoping to see Dieter's other watcher. He did not see him. He looked again.
He dropped his spoon and Rachel saw the color drain
from his face.

"What's the matter?"

"Over there, in the back of the café, at a table by himself. Look quick, then turn your back."

Rachel did. There, sitting in a corner across the room,
polishing off a big breakfast, was Mueller, his sunken
cheeks barely recognizable with his mouth full of eggs.
He seemed unaware he was being observed. Rachel
hoped it was so.

□□□ 32 ∎

EDDIE LOOKED about the shop, an elegant place filled with expensive-looking furniture, each surface with an artful display of small objects. Eddie merely glanced at the contents, and instead tried to see through the open door at the rear of the store. He was lining up exits to use in case of an emergency. He could see, just inside the door, a stairway leading up and another going down. A short, bald man wearing a pinstripe suit and a silver tie approached from the back room and asked, in German, if he could be of any help.

Eddie made a quick—and as usual accurate—estimate of the man's character. This one could be easily intimidated. Eddie slowly removed his wool-lined raincoat, folded it over his arm, and spoke.

"I'm here in Berlin on a buying trip. I'm a decorator. I have need of a great many things, and only a small amount of time to buy them. Are you the owner?"

"No, but I think I can help you," the salesman said in perfect English. "We have a lot of American customers."

"I see. Is the owner on the premises?"

"Yes."

Eddie turned, as though to ignore the salesman. "Then I shall only speak to him. I'm sorry, but as I said, I'm in a rush to make a great many purchases."

"Very well, sir. I'll see if he's available." It worked. The salesman left the room. While he was gone, Eddie browsed near the street-front window, looking to see if either of Dieter's men was visible. He saw one, idly inspecting a display in a window across the street. The man looked up and saw Eddie. Eddie quickly turned away and looked at his watch. Four minutes until Jeffrey and Rachel made their move.

"My name is Derek Wingill-Hunt. I am the owner of this store." Eddie turned and saw a tall, austere Englishman, about fifty years old, looking down at him. "My salesman said you wish to speak to me. I'm sorry, but I'm short of time this morning. It will have to be done quickly."

Wingill-Hunt had piercing blue eyes, a patrician manner, and was clearly interested in having Eddie do his business and leave as quickly as possible. Eddie went for it without much of a preamble.

"Mr. Wingill-Hunt, my name is Edward Alvarez the Third." He did not offer his hand in greeting. "I was going to say I was a decorator from Los Angeles looking to buy several roomfuls of expensive antiques. But that, as the quaint American expression goes, is pure bull-pucky. I am, in fact, an officer of the Los Angeles Police Department and I am looking for something modern."

"We have nothing more modern here. Good day." Wingill-Hunt made a dismissive nod toward the door.

"Oh, yes you have. As a matter of fact, you have had it for only a few hours. The truck brought it over from East Berlin early this morning. I think we should talk."

Wingill-Hunt stiffened, then tried to hide his reaction.
"My office is upstairs, Mr. Alvarez. Perhaps we
should talk."

"We will talk right over here, near the window." Eddie stepped toward the window, making sure he could be
seen from the street. "This is an ugly business you're in,
Mr. Wingill-Hunt. People are being killed so that you can
exchange your forgeries for good art. I presume the
Frank Stellas have all come back here to what the art
magazines are calling the burgeoning Berlin art market."

"Go on, Mr. . . . Mr. . . . ?"

"Alvarez. I'm a detective."

"A bit off your patrol, aren't you?"

"Not at all. I have a proposition for you. One you
won't be able to refuse."

"Oh?"

"Right. Your free-lance terrorist, Mueller, is about to
fly off to New York with a new shipment. I suppose you
have some clever way of getting it through customs. I
don't yet know what that is, but I'm going to find out."

At the mention of Mueller, the patrician look disappeared and the eyes turned hard. He said nothing.

"Mueller will make it to New York, but he won't get
outside the airport unless we talk. What we are going to
talk about is this." The salesman was edging his way toward the door at the rear of the shop. Eddie saw him.
"Get back in here. There are people watching this building, and if you try anything you're in deep shit. You understand deep shit, don't you?"

Both the salesman and Wingill-Hunt nodded.

"I always thought you high-class Englishmen had a
great sense of fair play. Well, so much for that. Sit
down," Eddie ordered. Both men sat, Wingill-Hunt on
the edge of a brocade-covered ottoman, the salesman ever
so delicately on a delicate Empire chair.

"I'm cutting myself and my partners in. Your East Berlin forgers may have to work a little bit harder, but I'm sure there will be enough money to go around. That is, if you want to stay in business."

"Mr. Alvarez, are you aware what happens to people like you? There are things that can be done."

"Shut up and listen. Two people are about to walk into this shop. A man and a woman. They are my partners. I have another one in New York, and he's just waiting for a call from one of us. Either you turn the art over to us, or you're out of business. And probably in jail."

"Blackmail." Wingill-Hunt now thought he understood.

"You've got it." Eddie heard footsteps on the floor above. "Are you alone here?"

"Yes, just the two of us," Wingill-Hunt answered evenly.

"Funny, but I don't believe you. Here come my partners." Eddie could see Rachel and Jeffrey crossing the street. When they walked in the store, he could see they were both terrified.

The salesman was cowering on his regal chair, and Wingill-Hunt sat rigid on his backless perch. Both obviously had hoped it was a ploy, and Eddie almost smiled at their crestfallen looks as Jeffrey and Rachel walked in the door.

Eddie introduced them as his partners. "You will be relieved to know that the professional level of your business has just gone up considerably. Miss Sabin owns an art gallery and has many connections in the art world. Mr. Dean is an antiquarian bookseller. And a journalist." Wingill-Hunt winced at that.

Jeffrey ignored the two sitting men and walked directly over to Eddie. He whispered in his ear.

"Mueller was in the café. He left just ahead of us and walked around the back. So I—"

"Secrets. I don't like secrets."

Eddie, Jeffrey, and Rachel all looked up. Standing in the doorway was Mueller. He had a gun, silencer in place, trained on them. The first shot hit Eddie squarely in the shoulder.

"AH, GOOD." Wingill-Hunt stood and dusted his knees as if the business at hand had been distasteful to him. "I dislike secrets too. I expect yours will accompany you to the grave, Mr. . . . . Mr. . . . ?"

"Dean." If he could have spoken without moving his lips, he would have done so. Rachel, who had been standing close to Eddie, now held him by his arm, helping him to remain upright. Eddie held his other arm in a grip he hoped was tight enough to slow the loss of blood. Once again, he looked out the window. This time he could not see either of Dieter's men. He was not a man given to despair, but he was feeling an unfamiliar emotion of hopelessness.

"We are not alone. There are others outside," Jeffrey said, looking out the window and wondering whether or not he should try to jump through it to attract their attention.

"Oh, a whole gang of blackmailers? Come now, Mr. Dean." Wingill-Hunt was oozing charm.

"Shut up, all of you. And listen," Mueller stepped forward and shoved the nose of his gun into Jeffrey's groin. "Otherwise, this nice-looking man will lose his balls. You first," he said, nodding at Eddie, "then the woman. Walk slowly through that door and start up the steps. I'll be right behind you with this man." He gave the gun a jerk upward for emphasis. Jeffrey stiffened, and somehow swallowed his cry of pain. They started for the back of the shop, then up the staircase.

"You stay downstairs," Mueller told the salesman in German. "Close the store."

They were taken upstairs to an elegant office that faced on the street below. Wingill-Hunt stepped to the two windows and closed the draperies. In a corner near the window were the forgeries, all neatly packed in tube-shaped shipping containers.

"Now, what is it you want?" Mueller asked evenly.

"He's a police officer, she owns a gallery," Wingill-Hunt began.

"I know about her. And this one too," Mueller said, smiling at Jeffrey. "Why a policeman?"

"I think you'd better stop right there," Eddie said. "We are here with a proposition. Cut us in, or close down your business."

Mueller laughed. Eddie began to sit, but Mueller jerked him back up.

"No laughing matter," Jeffrey said. "Either you cut us in or you'll never get back into the United States. We know you're leaving in a few hours. But if anything happens to us, it's the end of the line for you too."

"Oh?"

"Try us," Rachel said. She could hear her voice crack with fear, and knew that her taunt was useless.

"I'm going to. It doesn't matter to me . . . or to him." Mueller looked at Wingill-Hunt, who was sitting behind an intricately carved desk. "You disappear. So what if we can't go back to the United States. You think you are the only people who buy art?

"Others will. Many others. You think the East German government is in on this, don't you? That's why all those CIA people are snooping around. Don't be stupid. This has nothing to do with politics. It goes on without you or people like you. There are lots of rich Arabs who don't know the difference between fake and real art. All they know is how to spend money. It's all arranged."

"Are the young Arab men all arranged for your pleasure?"

Mueller answered Jeffrey's question instantly, hitting him hard on the shoulder with the butt of his gun. Jeffrey fell. Rachel begged for him to stop.

"Ah, that's right. This is your man," Mueller looked down at Jeffrey. "So you know I like men. Stand up. Take off your clothes."

"What?"

Mueller repeated his instructions without a word. He did it—twice—with the butt of his gun. Jeffrey stood painfully and began removing his clothes. They all watched. Eddie and Rachel hid their quiet desperation as well as they could. Wingill-Hunt grinned with pleasure. Mueller's smile filled out his sunken cheekbones. Jeffrey stripped—slowly—to his shorts.

"Your underwear too."

Jeffrey's final defense fell in a heap around his ankles.

"I'm going to fuck you when I kill you, just like I did your friend." Jeffrey said nothing, and looked—pleadingly—at Eddie. Rachel began to cry, as much for Jeffrey as for Henry. Mueller circled Jeffrey, touching him lightly. Jeffrey closed his eyes, and his ears were pounding. He nearly missed it.

Rachel and Eddie heard it first, the sound of soft footfalls on the carpeted stairs. Mueller heard it as well. Wingill-Hunt pulled a gun out of his desk drawer and headed for the door. He was shot the instant he pulled it open.

Mueller, who had been standing in front of Jeffrey inspecting his prize, momentarily lost his advantage when he turned to watch Wingill-Hunt open the door. Jeffrey jumped him from behind, and Eddie fell on him too.

Mueller's gun went off as it slipped from his grasp. The bullet struck a seventeenth-century portrait of a German nobleman in his elegant robe. Mueller scrambled up and ran from the room. Jeffrey and Eddie heard a shot, then the sound of a body slamming against the staircase wall. Running footsteps followed immediately. Jeffrey chased after Mueller, jumping over Wingill-Hunt, who was slumped in the doorway, a puzzled look on his face and blood flowing from his chest.

He stopped at the door, immobilized by the sight of a gun trained on him and a shouted order in German. The agent was startled to see a naked man standing before him, and it took a second for Jeffrey to come to his senses and tell him he was after Mueller too. Jeffrey ran down the stairs and into the shop, Rachel right behind him.

The shop was empty, but they could see bloodstains leading through what had been the crowded display of antiques. Now they were scattered, many broken. Mueller's exit had not been a neat one.

Jeffrey ran out the door into the freezing air. Rachel kept up with him easily. Mueller, bleeding profusely from his leg, was sitting on the sidewalk beside the curb. Two agents had guns on him while a third handcuffed him. The salesman was already handcuffed and sitting in a car. Cantwell, unwrinkled and apparently undistressed, stood beside them.

"Where's Dieter?"

"I don't know."

"You said he was inside when you called."

"I know." Jeffrey smiled. "I thought that would get you here real fast." He stopped and let the lie sink in. "There's a wounded man upstairs. Two, in fact. One of them is ours."

"Where the hell is Dieter?"

"I don't know."

"What do you mean you don't know? You said he was here!"

"I lied." He looked quickly up and down the street and decided the arrival of Cantwell's men had scared off Dieter's two watchers.

Cantwell could barely contain his fury. A crowd had formed on the street. Jeffrey suddenly realized he was standing stark naked in the middle of Keithstrasse.

"Give me your coat," he said to Cantwell. Rachel was already struggling out of hers.

Cantwell had been deceived, and like most deceived men his first instinct was to inflict humiliation. He made no move to take his topcoat off. "You look a bit uptight."

"You would be too if you had any." Jeffrey turned and started back toward the shop. Rachel put her coat over his shoulders. It served no real purpose but it did make her feel better.

They found Eddie, shirtless, being treated by one of Cantwell's men.

"They stop Mueller?" Eddie asked as Rachel and Jeffrey walked in the room.

"Yes," Rachel said, smiling. "He's been shot in the leg. Cantwell's people have him."

"Cantwell? Where did he come from?"

"When we saw Mueller in the café, I panicked," Jeffrey said, pulling on his underwear. "I called Cantwell and told him we had Dieter here in this office. I figured it would get him here real fast."

"And it did," Rachel said. Eddie laughed, then winced with pain.

While Jeffrey dressed, Rachel unwrapped one of the forgeries. She pulled the print from the tube and carefully unrolled it on the floor. "Look at this," she said, standing back to admire it. It was from Frank Stella's *Had Gadya* series, a bright, boisterous copy of *The Butcher Came and Slew the Ox*. It was a perfect—as near as Rachel could tell—copy of the same print that was hanging on the wall of their living room half a world away.

"God, I don't think my feet will ever warm up." Jeffrey was rubbing furiously, trying to restore circulation to his feet. "Talk about embarrassing . . ."

"You have more to warm than your feet." Eddie looked at Jeffrey. It was a look of respect and humor.

A team of German paramedics walked into the room and stopped first at Wingill-Hunt, who was still slumped in the doorway. Another went immediately to Eddie. It became a big crowd in a small room as more medics arrived, followed by Cantwell. Wingill-Hunt was alive— barely—and was quickly taken to a hospital. Eddie followed seconds later, vowing to return to the hotel within hours.

"Now tell me about Dieter." Cantwell sat in the polished leather chair behind the desk as if he had a prior claim to it.

"Nothing to tell," Rachel said. "Eddie—"

"I've found out about Eddie. He's a cop with a mission." Cantwell's disdain was almost palpable.

"We could use more like him," Rachel said before continuing. "Eddie was already in here when we saw Mueller. Jeffrey and I wanted help. Otherwise, it wouldn't work—and it was much too dangerous."

"What wouldn't work?"

Rachel explained.

"Dieter helped you find this place?"

"Yes." Jeffrey now had his shoes and socks on, and his dignity intact. "Look, you only want Dieter. We want—wanted—something else. It seems we have what we call a conflict of interests."

"It might also seem you were acting against the interests of your government, and against specific instructions I gave you."

"What you didn't tell us is even more significant," Rachel said. "We came here to find Dieter. We believed he was the man who murdered Henry, and the other people. And that he was dealing in forgeries. You knew all along he wasn't the murderer or the forger, didn't you?"

"Yes. And I also knew he was looking for the forger too. I figured you'd find each other—and I'd find Dieter."

"Part of your plan worked anyway." Jeffrey looked directly at Cantwell, and hoped he sounded reasonable. There was no sense in provoking him now, and besides, he wasn't really the enemy.

□□□ 34 ■

SMOG HANGS like a shroud over most of Berlin in the
late months of winter. East Berlin, without the resources
of the West, warms on coal, and pollutants travel across
borders, walls, and philosophies without restraint. The
air was dirty and the sun obscured and disappearing
quickly as Rachel, Jeffrey, and Eddie once again walked
through the no-man's-land at Checkpoint Charlie. They
were unaware of the grim sky above them and looked for
all the world like three tourists. They wanted it that way.
Even Eddie, whose arm was in a sling and whose senses
were slightly dulled by the last of the painkillers, had
about him an uncharacteristic exuberance. They crossed
without fear and with much curiosity. They had a mission of sorts, and were about to visit an ally—of sorts.

They showed their passports, then walked out of the
narrow hall into the inspection room. On the way out
Eddie bumped his arm on the narrow doorway. He issued a stream of epithets in Spanish.

"Translation?" Jeffrey asked.

"You wouldn't want to hear it," Eddie responded. "Spanish is a great language for swearing."

Dieter was waiting for them in the inspection room. They greeted him cordially, and a bit formally because of the curious Vopos standing around the room. Dieter escorted them out a side door and past a rack of large mirrors on metal poles used for looking under vehicles crossing the border. A car waited. It was a Russian-made car, spacious but noisy, the engine emitting a sharp whine as it bounced over the rubble in the road and continued on into East Berlin.

Jeffrey looked out as they headed down Marx-Engels-Platz toward the television tower, the Pope's Revenge. It stuck out of the surrounding architecture with such misplaced prominence that it was impossible to ignore. East Berlin, Jeffrey thought to himself, the city with an erection—and no place to put it.

Ten minutes later, they were weaving through a series of side streets along the Spree. Jeffrey recognized the warehouse the moment he saw it.

"Here we are," Dieter said as he left the car. "I promised you'd all see it—Mr. Dean from the inside this time—so that you could admire the German Democratic Republic's fine trained workmanship."

Dieter took out keys, unlocked the door, and walked inside ahead of them. Rachel walked immediately behind Dieter, through a small, dirty, and abandoned office onto the floor of the warehouse.

Spread out in one corner was the printing facility. A large, flat marble-topped table contained a print-in-progress.

"Hockney," Rachel said as she looked at it. She bent closer. "And well done at that." She looked closer. "Almost a perfect impression."

Jeffrey was squatting, peering up inside the machinery

of the press bolted to the floor. "So David Hockney was the next artist to be forged."

"Yes," Dieter said. "And here are some original works, the ones being copied. These are skilled professionals." Dieter pulled out a drawer and carefully placed four Hockney prints on the marble. Like the Stellas, they were brilliantly colored.

"I should tell you about the forgers," Dieter said.

"Where are they now?" Eddie asked.

"Back in prison, probably plying their trade." Dieter would have preferred to omit this part, but he had promised his part of the story and intended to keep his word. "The three men who were being paid by Wingill-Hunt to forge the prints were trained forgers. There is a prison, not far from here, where the prisoners are taught the fine art of forgery. It was begun by the Russians, and they still make use of it. It's a place where documents can be legally forged for whatever purpose the government needs them.

"False passports, identity papers, forged documents. Anything can be made at Bautzen. The better the forger, the better the forgery."

"How enlightened," Rachel remarked.

"That's one way of looking at it." Dieter smiled politely.

"This is state-of-the-art equipment," Eddie said, inspecting the press. "Must have cost a small fortune."

"Probably. Wingill-Hunt paid for it out of his thriving antique business. From the start it was lucrative. Labor costs are a lot lower here. Mueller set it up. He was the *Grenzgänger* . . . the border crosser."

"Like you?" Jeffrey remembered Dieter had described himself as a *Grenzgänger*.

"Yes, but my reasons for crossing were different."

"Have you ever . . ." Rachel paused, wondering if

she should even ask. "Have you ever considered crossing for one last time?"

"You mean defect?"

"Yes."

"No, it does not occur. At least not to me. I think that's why I'm allowed to cross as I like. They know I will return."

"Why?"

"That could be a long conversation. I am a German. I was born in this city . . . in this part of the city. I belong here, and I will remain here. That may sound a bit . . . a bit simplistic, but not if you understand the German character."

They continued to look over the presses for several moments. As they turned to leave, Dieter paused, thought a moment, then walked to the marble table. He picked up the completed Hockney forgeries, rolled them carefully, and took them with him as they left the building.

"What will happen to the presses?" Jeffrey asked as they drove away.

Dieter looked at his watch. "In about six hours, there will be a fire at the warehouse. Unexplained, at first, and then it will be discovered to have been caused by a defective electrical system. The warehouse, of course, will be saved."

"And that will be that," Eddie said softly.

"Yes. Except that Cantwell will not have the prisoner he hoped to have."

"That is your business and his," Jeffrey said. "We are not part of it."

"Well, not any longer," Eddie nodded.

Dieter laughed. "I have a message for you to deliver. That is if you'd like. Cantwell believes Wingill-Hunt was one of our people. He is not. He has lived in Berlin for years, and has dealt in antiques for just as long. He began forging antiques some years ago, a little here, a little there. It is a thriving business—over there." Dieter nodded in the general direction of the West. "Then he met Mueller. Actually, he didn't meet Mueller, he fell in love with him. At the time, Mueller was a student radical. He worked primarily for the Russians and for several Arab terrorist groups. The rest you can gather."

"Mueller won't be around for Wingill's pleasure any more."

"Mueller won't be around at all," Dieter said evenly. "He is a terrorist, and he knows things. Things about matters sensitive to the governments of our allies. The Soviets trained him and I believe they still employed him from time to time. This is not always a pleasant world. Mueller died in his hospital room this afternoon."

"With a little help," Eddie said, looking at Dieter.

"I cannot comment on that," Dieter said. "It is not my business. As I said, this is not always a pleasant world."

"By the way," Eddie said, "we have the answer to how Mueller exchanged the Stella belonging to Rachel. It took a couple of telephone calls back to Los Angeles, but in the end Henry's secretary had the answer. She recalled that Henry had been visited at the museum by a man who said he was a curator of modern art for the New National Gallery. It was Mueller. He fits her description perfectly."

"She said he spent several hours at the museum, and then went out to dinner with Henry," Jeffrey added. "She remembered it exactly. She even made the dinner reservation. That's when she met him—for about a minute. He had no appointment, so she had no note of it."

"The night Henry was murdered." Rachel spoke softly. The others had to lean toward her to hear.

"Ample time to make the switch," Eddie continued. "Henry Thurmond accidentally helped. The secretary said the print was already out of its old frame and in a folder in Henry's office."

Dieter thought for a moment of making an expression of sympathy, but decided it might appear insincere coming from him. His companions, these inadvertent co-conspirators, knew he had seen far too much to be distressed about the death of a man he had never known.

"And Wingill-Hunt?" Rachel wanted to change the subject.

"That's up to the courts to decide," Dieter was quick to answer. "He means nothing, and I think he will face the consequences of his actions."

"If he lives," Rachel said quietly.

They had arrived back at the checkpoint. A Vopo, his machine gun slung across his shoulder, approached the car. Dieter spoke to him in German, then pulled his wallet from his breast pocket to show his credentials. The car drove up to the first barricade.

Rachel, Jeffrey, and Eddie said polite farewells to Dieter, and then Rachel remembered something.

"The address you gave me in New York. Can you be reached through it?"

"Yes."

"Then your Grosz print will be along as soon as I get back to Los Angeles and pack it up."

"That isn't necessary."

"Yes it is." Rachel smiled at him. "You bought it, and I believe you do admire Grosz. I think you share his love of this city."

"I admire him very much. And thank you. I shall keep it as a souvenir of meeting all of you."

Dieter turned and walked to the rear of the car. The

driver followed him and opened the trunk. Dieter withdrew the four Hockney prints he had removed from the
warehouse. One he placed back in the trunk.

The other three he rolled individually and handed to
Jeffrey, Rachel, and Eddie.

"A memento for each of us."